Amelia's War

Dunham - 01

ANN RINALDI

SCHOLASTIC INC.

New York Toronto London Auckland Sydney
Mexico City New Delhi Hong Kong

ISBN 0-590-11745-9

12 11 10 9 8 7 6 5   0 1 2 3 4/0

Printed in the U.S.A.   40

First Scholastic printing, March 2000

The text type was set in 13-point Adobe Caslon.
Book design by David Caplan

To Mary Baykan and John Frye

of the Washington County Free Library

and to Roger S. Keller

for all their help and support

How the War Started for Me and What I Determined to Do About It

One day in August of 1861, Mama and I were invited to tea. That's how the war started for me. At Mrs. Gruber's in Williamsport. A farewell tea for Dewitt Clinton Rench, the handsomest young man in Washington County. I'd always thought him dashing. All the girls did. Even in his Confederate uniform, as he was that day when he was shot down on the streets of Williamsport for being a Rebel.

Mama and I were Southerners, but not Rebels. We were for the Union, but not the Yankees. You have to be from Maryland to understand it. Mrs. Gruber was a Rebel, but we were invited because she and Mama had always been friends. We were all still neighbors who'd known each other forever, and nobody knew yet how to draw the lines.

Tea and Mrs. Gruber's scones and iced lemon cake

in her front parlor. Girls who looked like iced cake in summer dresses, hoop skirted, bumping into each other, whispering about Dewitt, and him loving it all. There he sat in a place of honor, all gussied up in his new cavalry uniform with the sash around his waist, the sword, and the hat turned up on one side with a feather. And those shiny boots. He was riding with Kyd Douglas, his friend from college. They'd both studied law. So civilized, all of it, I wished he'd joined our side.

In the midst of the chatter and admiring whispers, another sound, soft at first but growing. Ugly. "Come on out, Dewitt. Stop hiding behind the ladies' skirts. Face the music. And it ain't Dixie."

Then stones against the house. And a window smashed. Dewitt stood up, bowed to us, and took his hat and his leave. His horse was out front, neighing in terror. We rushed to the windows to see him mount her.

Mobs in Williamsport are the same as mobs in Hagerstown, where I live. Daddy says they are centipedes, one head and many legs. As Dewitt mounted his beautiful bay mare, the fuss got louder. The mob wouldn't leave off. They just kept having at it, saying the most insulting things. I guess Dewitt couldn't abide it any longer. He turned and fired shots over their heads. Nobody was hit, but then just as Dewitt got to the Odd Fellows Hall, a man grabbed his horse's reins.

Dewitt fired down, shooting the man in the bootstrap. Then came another shot — nobody to this day knows from where. But Ed Steffey, the druggist, said they saw a man fire his gun from an alley, and Dewitt fell to the ground, shot in the back.

Up to then I guess everybody thought that what happened at Fort Sumter in April could still be patched up. By then, of course, Maryland had come out for Mr. Lincoln and the Union. He needed us. Up to then it had all been parades, speeches, and the Home Guards forming up. Our young men had gone both ways, most with the Union.

Mama and I left the Grubers' as soon as Dewitt went down. Mama wanted away from there. "We're going home and sealing up the doors and the windows," she said. I went along with her until we got back to Hagerstown, then I just don't know what came over me. I made Mama stop the wagon in front of the office of the *Hagerstown Mail*. I couldn't stand it. My heart was bursting. I was hot all over, then cold. My stomach was turning. I'd never eat again. Dewitt had been a *friend*! Some of the people in that mob had watched him grow up! I jumped out of the carriage and ran into the newspaper office to sob my story out to Mr. Dechart.

"Wrong," I wailed, sitting in the swivel chair while he fetched me a glass of water. "Wrong to shoot somebody down just because they stand for what they believe in!"

Mr. Dechart was hard put to becalm me. But after a while, he did. Then he fetched pencil and pad and told me to tell him all about it again. Just how it happened. So I did. He wrote it down, thanked me, and walked me out to Mama, who was waiting in the wagon.

"You've got a brave little girl here," he told Mama. "Most people would just head for home and shut the doors and windows."

Mama sat very straight, holding the reins. "It's what I wanted to do, Mr. Dechart. But Amelia wouldn't have it. I'm afraid she has my mother's tendencies. Mama's been part of the Abolitionist movement in Philadelphia, you know."

Mr. Dechart nodded. "I have Southern leanings, Mrs. Grafton, but right is still right and wrong is still wrong, and Amelia here knows it. I thank her. I shall write an editorial."

He not only wrote an editorial, he put it on the front page. And he printed a special edition to do it. The editorial said something about "unfeeling, cold-blooded, money-sucking Yankees."

We had no money-sucking Yankees in Hagerstown

or Williamsport, as far as anybody knew. Never mind. One day later Confederate troops camped across the river from Williamsport, wanting to torch the town without further ado. But their officers managed to keep calm.

Two days later my older brother Wesley came into my room grinning, and threw a copy of the other Southern paper in town, the *Torch Light*, on my bed.

There it was on the front page. Mr. Dechart had been arrested for "Southern leanings" in his writing and sent to Federal prison in Washington City.

Wesley grinned. "Gotta hand it to you, Amelia. Here we all are, running around, trying to figure out what we can do for the war effort, and you've already done something. Congratulations!"

He was astonished. And there wasn't much I could do to astonish Wes.

In school and on the street, pro-Union people stopped me, congratulated me, once word got around that I'd given Mr. Dechart the story that led to his arrest. I kept my head down, mumbled words even I didn't mean. I hadn't intended for this to happen! What would happen now to the *Hagerstown Mail*? To Mr. Dechart's son, Josh? He went to school with my brothers and his mother was dead. He was practically an orphan, with his father gone. Everybody wondered.

What happened was Josh quit school and tried to keep the paper going. But he was only twelve. He had to suspend publication.

All because I had to open my big mouth. Stand for something. Declare myself. And try to be like Grandmother Schuyler in Philadelphia, who'd founded the Philadelphia Vigilance Association to aid colored persons in distress, before I was born.

Why couldn't I be like other girls my age, content to wrap bandages or make lemonade and cookies when the Home Guards formed up? Well, I wasn't.

Mama didn't say much. Daddy owned and ran a general store in town. He was in the Washington County Businessmen's Association with Mr. Dechart. "I think perhaps a sojourn from Grandmother Schuyler's influence is due," was all Daddy said.

I was crushed. I was supposed to leave the following week. I looked forward to my summer visits with Grandmother Schuyler. Something was always happening in Philadelphia. They had real theater there, libraries, bookshops. Grandmother was always having a tea for some important personage.

Mama and Daddy argued over it, one of the few times they had words. Mama thought I should be allowed to go to Grandma's. "We always said we wanted our daughter to be a thinking person!" But Daddy held firm.

In six weeks Mr. Dechart came home from prison, took the oath of allegiance to the Union, and softened his editorials. Josh couldn't forgive him, and he and his father had a bad falling out. That's what Wesley said. I always liked Josh Dechart. When I went to watch him and my brothers play Rounders in the lot on the edge of town, he was polite to me. With his red hair, spectacles, and knowledge of newspapering, Josh was always listened to by the other boys. And once or twice he even took the side of us girls when the boys didn't want to let us try to hit the ball. But I never could understand his feelings about his father. Poor Mr. Dechart. Daddy said the Federals were always watching, even though he took the oath.

Then, in May of '62, when the Rebels won at Front Royal in Virginia, a mob decided to take it out on Mr. Dechart. They had to punish somebody, didn't they? So they wrecked the *Hagerstown Mail* office, including Mr. Dechart's pride, the Washington Hand Press.

There was something terribly wrong about that. Everybody in town knew it as they went to view the wreckage. "It's like some sacred covenant is broken among the townspeople," Mama said. "You don't destroy printing presses in America. You don't stop a man from printing what he thinks, even if he disagrees with you."

But they had. And again I blamed myself for starting it.

Mama said somebody else would have told Mr. Dechart about the shooting if I hadn't. But most of the people who were at that tea were wishy-washy, prissy boots women. And the men outside — well, forget them. Mama wasn't above reminding me, either, that the establishments of other Rebel sympathizers in town were also attacked. Rhodes' Restaurant, Mr. Gruger's silversmith shop. As if it helped.

The difference is that a newspaper has a soul. I've learned that since.

Mr. Dechart left town. Just disappeared. Josh wouldn't go with his father. So he lived in the abandoned newspaper office like a hermit, trying to fix the ruined Washington Hand Press. Even though he quit school, he was smarter than anybody I knew. And I ought to know, because I brought him food sometimes. I did this to make up for what I'd done. He wouldn't hear of it, of course.

"Each person is responsible for his or her own actions," he told me. That's why I liked him — he included women in things. Sometimes I think I learned more from him than I did in my stupid school.

But one thing I learned on my own. To keep my nose out of things in that terrible war. Just hunker down, like some people around here, and wait for it to be over. Because Mama was wrong. I'm not like Grandmother Schuyler. When you take sides, somebody most always gets hurt. Why did Grandma never tell me that? I just don't have the mettle for it.

We had a saying in Hagerstown, that the war comes to each of us in its own way and its own time. And so that's how it came to me. And this is what I determined to do about it.

Nothing. I decided then and there. No more would I put myself forth. Never again.

CHAPTER ONE

How I Didn't Get to Go to Philadelphia — Again

SEPTEMBER 10, 1862

Everything was packed.

Hard to believe you can pack up all the merchandise in a general store in one morning, but we did it. All of us worked together, me and Mama, Daddy, my brother Wes, home from St. James College for the occasion, even my little brother, Sky. Aunt Lou organized the packing. Mama oversaw things.

I marked the crates — *stoneware, pots, calico, glassware, hard candy* — in my best penmanship. I'd won a prize for it in school. A silk parasol. I had the best penmanship in the family. Daddy often asked me to write up the prices of things when he wanted to list them in the store.

Aunt Lou couldn't write. She was a freed slave, up from Virginia. She had come to us the previous May with dozens of other refugees, bearing a letter, right after the Confederates won the battle of Front Royal. She'd been sent by a woman who was some degree of kin to Daddy. "Not safe for her here," the letter said. "She's a real treasure, well-versed in the science of herbs and lotions. And a powerful good cook."

We'd never had negra help. At first I didn't know how to act around Aunt Lou. She'd once been a *slave*. I spent a lot of time in the kitchen watching her, looking for signs of it, feeling sorry for her. I soon discovered that she didn't want my sorrow. Didn't need it. What she needed was me out of the kitchen, out of her way. She ran the place like she'd been running places forever. She had more mettle than ten white women. I'd never be as sure of myself as Aunt Lou. At first I thought it was because of how she cooked. She made the best beaten biscuits and fowl with mushroom sauce I ever tasted. I soon learned it was something else.

One day, she decided I needed a tonic. It was her cure-all, made from vinegar, with nails and iron filings in it. Vile stuff. Just looking at the bottle guaranteed you'd get better.

I gagged on it, but got it down. "How'd you get the way you are?" I asked.

"What way's that, chile?"

"So sure of yourself."

She'd laughed. "Jus' keep goin'. Put one foot ahead

of the other. No matter what happens. Soon people think you know what you're about, and follow."

I'd follow her anywhere, but I couldn't now. Now she was going North. To Philadelphia with Daddy. To Grandmother Schuyler's house. I hadn't gone again this summer. The war, Daddy said. It was a poor excuse. The war was coming here, not going there.

Confederates were coming to Hagerstown. General Lee was bringing his army North for the first time. A peddler had come through last night with the sad intelligence. And that's why we were packing. Daddy was known as a staunch Union man, so he had to leave. Aunt Lou, being a freed negra, could be taken by the Rebels and sold back into slavery.

I was seething because I couldn't go. At breakfast I'd had a regular hissy-fit, had to be sent from the table. "The second summer in a row I wasn't allowed to go to Grandma's!" I shouted. "And I can't go on this trip, either!"

"Your mother needs you here. I'd hoped you were old enough to know that," Daddy said, ushering me into the kitchen to eat. "And you have school."

"I'd learn more at Grandma's than at school!" I stamped my feet, wanted to throw things. "You just don't want Grandma to give me any more notions. Think I don't know it?" My heart was breaking for what I'd miss in Philadelphia: theater, bookstores, Grandma's abolitionist meetings. This autumn Lucretia Mott was to be a speaker at one of them. And she for women's rights!

"Grandma will love you!" I told Aunt Lou. "Her and her Underground Railroad! She's a conductor. You know that? I've met some people she sent on to Canada. Nothing like that happens here in Hagerstown. It's dull, dull, dull."

Daddy frowned at me. "I thought you didn't want to be involved with the war after the Dechart affair."

As always, he'd caught me up short. "I'm not talking about war, I'm talking about culture!"

"Are you sure?" He'd given me a funny look. "At any rate, we do not talk about Grandmother Schuyler's secret activities. Ever. Now eat your breakfast. I'm ashamed of you."

He'd gone on being ashamed all morning while we packed. I felt his silence like a slap. Outside on the streets, there were wagons full of people leaving, on their way to Clear Springs to go on up the mountain with their animals and household goods. Inside we'd been working since eight. I felt the ending of things, like we were packing all our good times into those crates and tagging them to be put away. I felt the beginning of things, too. Fear. Terror, if I let it become that. My father was leaving, war was coming, and he was put out with me. I knew this was wrong but didn't know how to right it.

Then, as I was making a crate of hard candy, he came and put a hand on my shoulder and spoke. "Do you remember the day Josh Dechart came into the store with a note from his father, when his class was visiting the newspaper office?" He turned to explain to Aunt Lou. "The note asked for a dozen jawbreakers. Josh put a zero after the twelve and made it a hundred and twenty pieces. I had no jawbreakers to sell in the store when he left!"

The recollection made everything worse. Was Daddy still punishing me? He knew my guilt about Josh. "Smart boy, that Dechart lad," he said. "Is he still living in the abandoned office, Amelia?"

I wasn't about to answer. Then Sky did. "He sure is. And Amelia goes to see him all the time. Sneaks there. With food."

"Schuyler!" Mama snapped. "We don't tell tales out of school in this family."

"Do you think it wise, Amelia? Going there?" Daddy asked.

He was a tall man, my daddy. He didn't wear a goatee, like so many men did. He was clean-shaven, and the cleanness of his face seemed to me to be an outward side of the cleanliness, the forthrightness that was inside him. He had dark hair that was thinning,

14

and what Mama liked to describe as "a high, intelligent forehead."

His blue eyes pierced into you. He had a slow way of speaking, with just a touch of the South about his accent that made you pay mind to every word, even if you didn't want to. Into those words went a lot of thought and meaning. He could make us feel small and lost and unloved without ever raising his voice.

"I'm the only friend Josh has these days, Daddy." I did my best to sound annoyed. "If this store was boarded up and Wesley was living here alone, wouldn't you want someone to visit him?"

"Wouldn't live here," Wesley said. "I'd go for a soldier first, if push came to shove."

"Hush, Wes," Daddy said. So Wes hushed. And Daddy considered my answer. He was always fair. If you stood your ground and thought your argument through, he'd be reasonable. "We have to be loyal to our friends," he said. "There are too many people watching each other like hawks, looking to besmirch the names of their enemies these days. And I have enemies."

"You mean like Mr. Wright?" Sky asked.

Mr. Wright owned the tavern next door. And he was part of the reason Daddy was leaving.

"Mr. Wright never was my good friend to begin with," Daddy said. "I loaned him money. He can't repay the loan, so he's decided to report me to the Confederates for a staunch Union man."

We all went back to our work. "Still say, if I were Josh Dechart, I'd go for a soldier," Wes said.

"Josh is too young, Wes," I told him.

"And so are you," Mama reminded him. Josh was my age, thirteen. Wes was sixteen.

"Besides, Josh hasn't taken sides," I added.

"Not taken sides?" My brother let out a hoot. "Everybody in town has taken sides."

"Not Josh," I said. "He wants to be neutral."

"A newspaper man? Neutral? They have leanings like the Tower of Pisa!"

I wanted to throw something at my brother then. A can of sardines, maybe. Hit him foresquare on the forehead. But I took the high ground instead. "He says good newspaper men in the future will have to be objective." I sounded as haughty as I could, but this only made Wes collapse with laughter.

"He's a Rebel," he said, "like his pa. They're all the same, him and his kind."

"So does that make me a Rebel because I'm his friend?"

He waved his hand in disgust. "You're a girl, what does that matter? Girls don't know their own minds. If they have any."

"Wesley Schuyler Grafton!" Mama glared at him. "We don't hold with such in this family. Are you saying that I don't have a mind?"

Then Daddy: "We encourage intelligent family discourse, but not flinging insults. Remember. And don't mouth off for the sake of hearing yourselves, either of you. This war was started by orators in the Deep South who loved the sounds of their own voices so much they just kept pushing and pushing until the fighting started."

"I'm not a Rebel," I told my brother. "And I don't side with them. I'm Josh's friend. I have a mind, but I'd just as lief sit the war out and not take sides, thank you."

"It isn't something you can sit out, like a dance." Wes's face clouded. He was serious, not taunting me. "It has to do with all of us. You can't sit it out."

He'd thrown the gauntlet on the floor, but I wasn't about to pick it up. Not about to make excuses why I'd refused to help Mama and other women make ready one of the new hospitals in town. Mama came over to me then and put her arm around me. "Enough chatter," she said, "let's get back to work now, or we'll never finish."

So we went back to work. Daddy was moving around the store, collecting some food and putting it in a basket. I thought it was to take with him on his trip, but then he brought the basket over to me. "Maybe you want to bring this to Josh," he said.

I looked in the basket. There were a couple of cans of sardines, some crackers and cheese, and some hard candy, the kind Josh liked so. There was also a small jug of cider. "Thank you, Daddy. He needs food." I took the basket, touched. It was his way of making up to me. I set it down and hugged him. I loved him, I did. He was so gentle and dear, and I didn't want him to leave.

"I thought Judge Alvey was looking after Josh," Mama said.

Judge Alvey had himself been arrested and sent to prison at the beginning of the war for favoring the South. He was released on the condition that he never enter a Confederate state, and that he mind his own business. Apparently the judge thought Josh was his business. "The judge and his wife send Josh food, Mama. And she has her washerwoman do up his clothes. But he'll be glad to know we're thinking of him, just the same."

"Food nourishes more than the body," Mama said. "That poor boy. You tell him any time he wants to sit down at the table with our family, he's invited, Amelia."

"I'll tell him, Mama, but he won't come."

"How soon before Lee comes?" Sky was sick of our mawkishness. He wanted to talk war. At ten he was crazed for it. His face was flushed with excitement. He didn't care what army came, as long as it was an army. Twice already he'd run off to visit encampments, once that of some Confederates who had spent the night this past July on the seminary grounds.

Daddy told him to go out the back door and see if the horse and wagon were here yet. Sky went. We finished up our work. "Some merchandise will have to be left here," Daddy told us. "There's no other way. Some medicines, jarred preserves, canned goods, pots, macintoshes, boots."

He was making small talk, awkward now at the thought of leaving.

"Do you want me to get the store windows boarded up, Wesley?" Mama asked Daddy.

"No. A boarded-up store invites vagrants. Anyway, I'll be back soon."

Sky came bounding in. "The wagon's here." He could scarce contain himself. "And both Jones boys with it."

"Oh, dear," from Mama. She didn't like the Jones boys. Cole and Travis, fifteen and sixteen, were wild. They'd left school in the sixth grade. The Joneses were no-count mountain people. Everybody knew that. They grubbed the land on a small spread outside town. But it wasn't for any of this that Mama did not like them. It was because she knew the Jones boys were fixing to run off and join the army, first chance they got. And Wesley had taken to running with them, lately.

"Now, Mother," Daddy said again, "they got us the wagon to save our things. And they said they'd take us to the Pennsylvania line tonight, too. You know there aren't any trains running out of town right now, there isn't a spare horse and wagon in fifty miles, and I can't leave you without the others."

Mama knew. Still, she sighed.

The Jones boys came in, grinned sassily at me, punched Wesley in the arm, and pulled Sky's hair. Then they carried the crates outside.

Mama, Daddy, and my brothers went out back to oversee the loading of the wagon. I stood watching my daddy giving instructions. The Jones boys would be around to our house later to pick up him and Aunt Lou. I knew my father didn't like going. It was running, no matter what name you put to it. But it was a passel better than staying and going to prison, like Josh's father. I slipped out the front door with my basket. Dust rose from the street as the steady stream of horses and wagons kept on coming on their way out of town.

The maples along the wood sidewalks filtered the

sun and gave it a mellow light. Josh's father had pro-
posed planting those maples in an editorial, the year
Josh was born. Everybody liked him and his ideas
well enough back then, didn't they? Now the trees
were a part of our town, like the railroad station and
the courthouse.

Wouldn't you know, the first person I ran into was
Lutie Kealhofer.

Lutie was difficult under the best of circumstances.
This morning she carried a long plume, the kind that
goes on a hat. "Why, hello there, Amelia Grafton."

"Hello, Lutie."

Her real name was Mary Louise. She was the
belle of Hagerstown. Her daddy was president of
Hagerstown Gas Light Company and her mama a
well-born lady. Both were ardent Confederate sympathizers. She was twenty-two now and betrothed to
Will Giles, Junior, who was in the Confederate cavalry. Will had graduated Princeton.

"Did you ever see the like?" She put a hand to her
eyes to shield the sun. "People leaving town in
hoardes. What are they afraid of?" She laughed. "I
just got back from visiting friends in Boonsboro.
Henry Kyd Douglas, that friend of Dewitt's, came
through this morning. He's with Stonewall Jackson.
The youngest on his staff. Douglas was going to stop

and see his parents, and the Federal cavalry fired on him. What is the world coming to when a cavalryman can't even pass through town on the way to see his parents? I can't imagine. A bullet tore this plume off his cap. I managed to retrieve it." She waved the plume in front of her face, and closed her eyes dreamily.

"Jackson's in Boonsboro?" I asked. Jinny Pearl Beale's father had a farm near there. She was Wes's sweetheart.

"Oh," Lutie waved the plume, "Jackson and the rest of them are gone now. Marched out this morning. Back across the Potomac, I hear."

"Then the Confederates are gone?"

"Not all of them." She smiled. "How is your family, Amelia? How are y'all?"

How should we be, I thought, with the Confederates all over the place, like fire ants. "We're fine, Lutie. What are you going to do with the plume?"

"Save it. And give it back to Kyd next time he comes through. I'm on my way to the drugstore for a soda. Would you like to come along?"

"No thank you, Lutie. Maybe next time. I've an errand to do."

"Well, you give my best to your mama now, you hear?"

I went on down the street, clutching my basket. I didn't like Lutie, but it wasn't because she was pro-South. I didn't like her because she thought herself too high-toned for the rest of us. But we Hagerstown people had a common past, our lives were fashioned out of the same fabric, so I might have to go for a soda with her one of these days. But not today.

The sign that said HAGERSTOWN MAIL hung half off its hinges in front of the newspaper office. The windows were boarded up. I knew Josh wouldn't answer a knock on the front door. I went through the alleyway that separated it from Jacob Wright's Tavern.

The same mob that had wrecked Josh's daddy's presses that terrible night the previous May went from there to Jacob Wright's Tavern and wrecked that establishment. Mr. Wright was a Southern sympathizer, too. But he'd been permitted to repair his place and go on. He only sold liquor. It spirited up the body. Not the mind, like Mr. Dechart's words did.

It made me sick what people would do in the name of patriotic duty. Mama said that since the war started there'd been enough fervor spent on feuds in this town, in the name of patriotic duty, to bring six more states into the Union.

Well, I can't say I did what I did out of patriotic duty. But look what happened anyway. I ruined things for Josh's father. Still, like Daddy said, Josh was one smart boy. He'd land on his feet. That was what everybody said about him.

Only I knew there was something broken inside him with all that had happened. You could hear it when you talked to him. Not in the things he said as much as in the things he didn't say. The spaces in the conversation. You could see it in his eyes.

Crazy as it sounds, I'd seen the same thing in Aunt Lou's eyes, never mind all her mettle.

I asked her about it once.

"Chile," she said to me, "chile. When bad things happen to us, sometimes we get broken inside. But that doan mean we can't be good again. And do more good maybe than those what ain't got somethin' broken inside. Sometimes us broken people can do great things. 'Cause they knows what's 'portant an' what ain't. You jus' give your friend time."

That's what she said. So I was giving Josh time. And I brought him food. And I went to visit him. Because I knew that someday Josh was going to do great things.

I was going to miss Aunt Lou. I wished she didn't have to leave with Daddy. I was going to miss her more than her beaten biscuits.

CHAPTER TWO

Of War and Old Wallpaper

We'd had troops here for over a year, ever since June of '61 when the first of the Union men passed through. We'd fed them, visited them, had them in our churches and our homes. They put their tents in our fields, their boots in our gardens, their horses and mules in the fields outside town. How many times we woke in the middle of the night to hear the tramp, tramp, tramping of their boots as they marched through town. They promised us all the time they wouldn't take things. Sure, and so do pigs have wings. They'd taken our fences for wood, our chickens for their soup pots.

Oh, they give us things, too. Smallpox for one. We had that in May of '61. Mama wouldn't let me or Sky out, even to go to school. And for a year now we've heard the distant rumble of shells the Union and Confederates lobbed at each other across the Potomac.

That's because we're a crossroads here, Daddy said. Southern generals saw Washington Valley as the Achilles' heel of the North. They could invade the North from here. Use South Mountain as a shield. Northern generals saw us as a place to make ready for the attacks into Virginia's Shenandoah Valley. They could both have it, far as I was concerned. I'd just as lief go to Philadelphia.

I knocked three times on the back door of the newspaper office, the signal appointed by Josh so he'd know it was me. The door opened and he stood there. He didn't smile. "You shouldn't be here," he said.

"Hello to you, too." I held out the basket. "I brought food."

His face softened. In looks he was not handsome. Too thin. His hair was bright orange-red, which is because on his mother's side they were Irish immigrants. But his eyes were brown, not blue. And he wore Benjamin Franklin spectacles, which made him look scholarly. At this time he was caught in that place between being a boy and a man. A bad enough place to be in good times. A terrible place to be in times of war.

His attire was clean enough. He was wearing the leather apron of a newspaper apprentice. His sleeves were rolled up, his hands filled with printers' ink.

"What are you doing?" I stepped inside and adjusted my eyes to the dimness.

"I've started salvaging the pica type."

I'd always loved the smells of the newspaper office, that of the ink, the paper. And then there was the sound of the press, so certain, bringing thoughts to life. I'd come many times to watch Josh and his father put the paper out.

Now I saw that the place had more order than the last time I was there. A lot of the debris was swept to one side. I saw that he'd been oiling the Washington Hand Press. I smelled the oil he'd been using. Where had he gotten it? How had he managed to repair the press? The judge, I thought.

"You're fixing things," I said. It was almost an accusation.

"Yes." He opened the basket of food. My father had sent a large piece of the orange mousetrap cheese, which Josh loved. Not to mention the crackers, sardines, and candy.

"Do you remember the candy?" I asked.

"'Course I do." He scowled. "Just goes to show you, Amelia. How you can change things with just a stroke of the pen."

Something told me he wasn't talking about the candy. I waited.

"That's what words are all about," he said, taking a bite of the cheese. "Changing things. Or just making people sit up and take notice. It's why I'm trying to fix the press. Between me and the judge, we think we might get things working again. We've got a club to use as a mallet to make proofs, and shackles to pound the type in place. That sawed-up board over there is to make a rack. You see how I've got the rods in the side posts bolted back on to the top and bottom beams?"

"Josh, do you mean to print the paper again?"

"Maybe."

"What for?"

He scowled. "Wouldn't you rather have a hundred and twenty pieces of candy instead of just twelve?"

"Well, yes, I guess."

"Well, then, wouldn't you rather have two viewpoints instead of just one?"

"Well, yes," I allowed.

"If we could compare viewpoints, maybe we could sit down and talk and not kill each other. That's what newspapers are all about. It isn't right to close one down just because the editor doesn't agree with you. That's not what this country is supposed to be all about, Amelia."

I hoped he wasn't serious about printing the paper again. How could he be, a boy of thirteen? How could he fix the press? I hoped it was just a result of being all cooped up in here by himself for so long. I watched him eat.

"Are you leaving, like everybody else?" he asked.

"No. My daddy is leaving. Philadelphia."

"To your grandmother's?"

"Yes, with Aunt Lou. Oh, I want to go so bad, Josh! I think it so unfair I'm not allowed to go again!"

"Guess you came home last time with too many seditious ideas."

That's why I liked him. He used words like *seditious*. The first time he used it, I had to look it up.

"You have to be careful about ideas. In places like Philadelphia, they're acceptable. Not here in Hagerstown."

That's why I liked him, too. He saw things the way I did.

"Why'd your father send the food?"

In ordinary company such a question would be ungracious. Not with Josh. He believed in asking questions. "He said we have to stick by our friends."

"Good of him. Tell him I'm beholden. I don't forget when somebody does me a good turn. But I don't think you should come by here when the Confederates arrive. It won't be safe."

"Why not?" I asked. "This paper always had Southern leanings."

He shrugged. "War is war. Sometimes such loyalties are forgotten. Sometimes all an invading army wants to do is destroy things."

"Do you think they'll really come, Josh?"

He shrugged. "People have been asking for a long time if Lee can carry the war north of the Potomac. Yankee gunboats have moved south to Baton Rouge, so I'd say he can get across and into Maryland."

"How do you know so much, Josh?"

"Don't know as much as I'd like. Especially now that the telegraph and mail are cut off."

"We know about the telegraph, but the mail, too?"

"The stagecoach left town this morning for its daily run to Frederick. A little while ago it came back. With the mail. And the same passengers."

He knew everything. And here I thought he was languishing away in the old place. All the while he'd been reading, for there was an assortment of books on a shelf. There was even a copy of the *Hagerstown Herald,* one of the Yankee newspapers in town.

"Josh, never mind the Confederates. The people of this town might put you in prison if you print the paper."

He smiled. "You ever hear about Oberlin, Ohio, in 1858?"

I sighed. "No." But I knew I was about to.

"Kentucky slave hunters were after a runaway slave. The people of Oberlin objected. Some of the slave's rescuers were put in prison. Two were printers. And they started a newspaper in prison. Newspaper people can't be stopped, Amelia."

"Newspaper people are crazy, too. Mama said that Mrs. Lincoln refers to them as the vampire press."

"I'd say, in Mrs. Lincoln's case, that's the pot calling the kettle crazy."

"I don't think you should say things against Mrs. Lincoln."

He shrugged.

I was scared for him. "Can you really print the paper again?" I asked.

"Only thing that's stopping me is no newsprint. They burned all my daddy had left. And you know the manufactory here in town wouldn't sell him any for a long while, anyway. Even the Yankee editors are running short now. They're cutting back on the size of their advertisements. I hear the newspapers down South are using old wallpaper to print on. You got any old wallpaper at your house?"

"No," I said. I didn't know if we had old wallpaper or not. I just didn't want to be responsible for him being thrown in prison.

He grinned at me. "Everybody has old wallpaper. Come on, Amelia, my press is almost fixed."

I looked down at my hands in my lap.

"Hey." He set down his cheese and crackers and peered at me. He was so eager and bright-eyed. He didn't have that Aunt Lou–look in his eyes now. He was his old self.

"You wouldn't be breaking any vow you made if you got me old wallpaper," he said.

I pulled away. "I took a stand once, Josh, and look what it did to you. Look at all this! Look at how you're living. I'll not be the cause of more trouble."

"Getting me some old wallpaper? You call that causing me trouble?"

"Yes."

"If you don't get it, the judge will give it to me."

I stood up. "Then let the judge give it to you."

He grabbed the edge of my skirt and looked up at me with that grin of his. "What about what your daddy said about sticking by your friends?"

I sighed.

"I need the wallpaper as much as I need food, Amelia. If you don't bring some around, don't bring food, either."

"That isn't fair."

"I'll tell you something that's even less fair. If I can't print the paper, then there's nothing more for me here. I might take it in my head to visit my uncle when he comes near here."

"Your uncle?"

"You remember, Colonel John McCausland of the 36th Virginia Infantry. He's bound to come by, sooner or later. I might take it in my head to join up."

"You're too young!"

"There's younger than me who are drummer boys."

"You're a pacifist. You said so yourself."

"I don't have to fight. Just gather information for him. Officers always need information."

His uncle, Colonel McCausland, was his dead mother's brother. "That's blackmail," I said.

"There can't be any blackmail between friends. Only friendship."

"Then you're persistent, Josh Dechart," I said. "I suppose it's that red hair of yours. Or your Irish ancestors on your mother's side."

"Does that mean you'll get me the wallpaper?"

"It means you're incorrigible." I looked down at him, so earnest. And so skinny! I knew if I didn't bring him food, he'd starve. What was worse, allowing him to starve? Or giving him wallpaper? "I'll look around home," I said, "and see if we have any."

"That's all I ask. Thanks, Amelia."

I said all right. I said I had to go. My daddy would soon be leaving. I'd be back.

"If you need anything, you know what to do," I said. We had a system. If he needed anything, he would write "traitor" in white paint across the boards of the front window. It had been written when the newspaper was ransacked.

I left. I hated going and leaving him all alone to sleep on a pallet with his gun. His Uncle John, the colonel, had sent it for his last birthday. It had a polished walnut stock. *Duckworth and Simmons, London, Established 1761* was imprinted on it. Josh said he would never use it unless he was attacked.

I said good-bye and went out the back door.

CHAPTER THREE

How Do You Bury the Past?

Two summers earlier, when I had last gone to Grandmother's, Daddy and Wesley built a Gothic washhouse for Mama. It was made of fieldstone and had darling little turrets. In one room were tubs, a cistern and a pump. There was also a sink and a fireplace with a proper iron crane that swung back and forth. This was where Mrs. Carmody did our wash. She came every Monday. On the second floor was a smokehouse and next door to the washhouse was the woodshed.

Our house was a mile from town at an end of a street that was shaded with big trees. All the houses there had wide porches and fenced-in yards. It wasn't Philadelphia, but if you had to live in Hagerstown, it was the best street. When I got home, my family was in the yard, near the washhouse. Daddy was putting his account books — his important records and legal papers, even some money — into a big iron wash kettle. On the side of the washhouse, where tall sunflowers grew, Wesley and Sky were digging a hole to bury everything in the ground. Our dogs, Duke and Duchess, sniffed around anxiously, knowing that something important was going on. Mama had her silver tea service on the ground. Daddy was urging her to wrap it in burlap and bury it, too.

"I won't," Mama said. "I just can't put it in the ground like that. It's so much a part of my life and my past. My great-grandmother brought it from England."

For as long as I could remember, that tea set had sat on Mama's sideboard in the dining room. I'd seen her lovingly polish it so many times. Mama didn't have notions or pretensions. She wasn't one for jewels or fancy clothes. But she loved that tea set inordinately.

"It'll soon be gracing the sideboard in some home in Richmond, if you don't bury it now, Leigh," Daddy said gently.

Mama didn't say anything. Into a big iron wash kettle went Daddy's things. There was room enough in it for the tea set. Daddy knelt on the ground looking up at her. "Well, Leigh?"

I saw tears in my mother's eyes. "I can't, Wesley. In

heaven's name, how can I bury my past? You know how Great-grandmother got this tea set here."

Daddy sighed patiently. He knew. We all did. We'd heard this story dozens of times. But Mama had to tell the story again.

"Her ship coming to America ran into a gale," Mama's voice recited. "Ran off course and had to drop anchor off the coast of Maine. It was spring. The only way to Boston was ox-drawn wagons. What roads there were were steeped in mud. Great-grandmother had to discard some of her things because the load was too heavy. She discarded her clothing, rather than this tea set. No, I shall not bury it, Wesley. Great-grandmother would haunt me if I did."

Daddy stood, cleared his throat, and signaled to Wes to cover over the hole. He and Sky shoveled dirt and sod over it. Then put a pile of wood on top.

"I've put several barrels of flour in the cellar," Daddy said. "As well as dried apples, potatoes, cheese, and sugar. Here's the keys to the store, Leigh. You know there's lots of goods left there."

Mama took the keys.

"Don't hand them over easily, Leigh. But don't endanger yourself or the children by not handing them over, either."

Mama nodded solemnly and stepped forward to

adjust his muffler. "The nights come quicker these days. And colder. I hate your traveling at night."

"It's the only way." Daddy looked at the sky. "We've still got a few hours of daylight." But the horizon was darkening and a brisk breeze was starting up. He glanced anxiously toward the street. "Where are the Jones boys? They're slower than General McClellan." Then he looked at Sky. "Go and tell Aunt Lou we're just about ready." His portmanteaus were at his feet. Sky ran to the house.

"One more thing, Leigh. Without Aunt Lou, you'll need household help. I was thinking of Jinny Pearl. What do you think, Wes? You think she'll come? I'll pay her two dollars a week and meals, and she can go home nights."

My brother wiped his hands on a piece of rag. "I can't comment on what Jinny Pearl's likely to do these days," he said. "When she's not reading books on Joan of Arc, she's firing that revolver of hers out in the field at imaginary Rebs."

"You two been fussing?" Daddy asked.

Wes lowered his eyes. "This war's got her so fired up, I don't know her anymore. But I'll ride over later and ask, if you want."

"No. She might say no just to spite you. Amelia can ride over."

Wes shrugged and turned away.

"I don't want you to plague your mother with any talk of running off to join the army when I'm gone, Wes," Daddy said. "I need you here, to look after things." The sound of wagon wheels came now from the street. "Hear me, Wes?"

"I hear," came the sullen answer.

"And you, Amelia, take care of your mother."

I nodded. Then everything happened at once. The wagon, driven by the Jones boys, came into the yard. Daddy hugged me, clapped Wes on the shoulder, and embraced Mama. I saw the look on his face when he pulled away. Like he'd been torn from her.

Aunt Lou came out of the house with Sky, lugging her portmanteau. "I left the fixin's for supper," she told Mama.

"You're a dear. I shall miss you." They embraced.

I hated Aunt Lou at that moment more than I knew I could hate. Because within twenty-four hours she would be sitting in Grandmother's kitchen in the elegant brick house in Philadelphia. She'd be hearing all that exciting talk, about war and the planning of the antislavery fair, held every year before Christmas. She'd be serving tea to important people, like the singer Elizabeth Taylor Greenfield, called the "Black Swan."

Oh, I hated her so! She reached out to embrace me. I held back, but then gave in, seeing the look on

Daddy's face and feeling ashamed. The Jones boys jumped out of the wagon and put in their luggage. Duke and Duchess started whimpering nervously.

Everything was hurdy-gurdy for a few seconds — dogs barking, called good-byes, horses turning to the street. And then we stood waving. And they were gone. Wes had all he could do to keep the dogs from following. A silence settled over us, terrible and pressing.

"Wes, you'd best get started on the evening chores," Mama said.

"It isn't evening yet." Then he saw the look on her face and started for the barn. Sky took the dogs and went with him.

"Amelia, you'd best ride over to Jinny Pearl's. Tell her tomorrow morning will do, if she'll have us."

How could my mother bear it? And then I thought of her mother, Grandmother Schuyler in Philadelphia, going against the grain of things to be an abolitionist. And her great-grandmother who'd thrown out her clothes rather than the tea set. I went to saddle up Pillow, my horse. And there, on the floor in the back of the barn, I found my brothers. Wes had a deck of cards and was teaching Sky to play poker.

"You're supposed to be doing chores," I said.

"You ever know a cow who wanted to be milked before four o'clock?" Wes asked.

I didn't, so I went about saddling Pillow. "You have any message for Jinny Pearl?"

"Yeah," Wes answered. "Tell her I'm going to do it before she does."

"Do what?"

"Never mind. She knows."

"Wes says Daddy's a coward for leaving," Sky piped in.

Wes reached out to smack Sky. "I said no such thing, you little snake. I said I wished he'd stayed instead. And faced them."

"It's the same thing." Sky held his arm where Wes had hit him.

I didn't know what Wes's problem was, but I was liking him less and less these days. "Daddy is the town treasurer, as well as a Union man," I said distinctly. "He isn't the only town official to leave."

"He should have made Ma bury the silver," Wes said.

"Everybody knows you can't make Mama do something if she hasn't a mind to."

"That's the trouble with women today," Wes mumbled.

Sixteen, and he thought he knew women. I was sick of him, sick of his swaggering, his sullen moods. But I said nothing. Outside the sun had disappeared. The sky was blackening. I led Pillow out of the barn.

Another wagon was pulling into the yard. I recognized Aunt Charlotte, the huckster. She wasn't really our aunt. Everybody in town just called her that. She sold flowers and vegetables. She was a plain woman, a widow and a Southern sympathizer. She got down from the wagon and came toward Mama.

"Saw your husband driving off. Figured you might need some fresh vegetables, Leigh."

"I might, Aunt Charlotte."

The two women stood taking each other's measure. The silver tea set sat on the ground between them. And I knew the exchange was about more than vegetables. "Come into the house and have some lemonade," Mama invited. "Amelia, be on your way." She picked up the tea service.

But Daddy's words, uttered not five minutes ago, still rang in my ears. "Take care of your mother."

"I'll fetch the lemonade first," I said. I tied Pillow to the hitching post and went inside.

CHAPTER FOUR

Secrets and Lies

I served them in the kitchen. Both the back and front parlors were used only for formal occasions. Having come from Philadelphia, Mama still held onto certain rules of society.

They sat at the oak table and sipped their lemonade and ate sugar cookies, like they were at a Methodist social. I hovered and waited, doing pretend-tasks and listening.

"I wanted to see the Southern army," Aunt Charlotte said softly, "but then my sister's boy rode over from Frederick this morning. Said they were the dirtiest bunch anybody'd ever laid eyes on. Not even with proper uniforms. Ragged and hungry looking. But they have a swagger about them, my sister's boy said, that the Northerners don't have."

"I'm sure they do," Mama agreed.

"Ride like circus-riders, he says. And some speak so funny, you can't even understand what they're saying."

"I'm sure they're like soldiers everywhere," Mama replied. "Brazen and showing off, but all scared inside. And likely hungry. My husband told me what it was like in the Mexican War, when he was so far from home."

Aunt Charlotte nodded, and said, "I heard that Mrs. Kealhofer already sent out an invitation to Lee to come for dinner when he gets here. But that he declined. Said he didn't want any retribution against the families who invited him after he and the army left."

"That was wise of him," Mama allowed.

The chatter went on. Aunt Charlotte knew all the gossip in town. Dr. and Mrs. Hauer had left that afternoon for her sister's in Pennsylvania. Everyone who had attended the Lutheran Synod at nearby Funkstown had left for home. Some people who had already seen General Lee had said his arm was in a sling. "Fell from a horse! Imagine! And him such a good horseman!"

Mama's tall case clock in the hall that came from Philadelphia struck the half hour. "Too bad the children can't start school," Aunt Charlotte said.

Mama agreed. "Sky needs the discipline." Sky went

to the private school kept by Mr. Hoffman. I went to the Red Brick School. It would be my last year there. Next year I'd be off to the Female Seminary. But with the fear of the Confederate invasion, the school year was put off.

A fly buzzed overhead. Outside I could see the sun slanting, but it was as if the world stood still, as if we were all waiting for something to happen.

The silver tea service sat on a side table by the wall, where Mama had set it down. I saw Aunt Charlotte eyeing it several times. What would Mama do if she up and said she wanted it? The woman was a Rebel, after all. Maybe now, with Rebs coming, she'd be brazen enough to take it. Maybe she had a revolver hidden behind that apron of hers. We'd known her for years. She'd always been more than fair in her dealings with Mama. Still. You couldn't tell about people, anymore. The war gave some of them the strangest notions.

What would I do? Let her have the tea set? Yell for Wes? He'd only chide Mama for not burying it. Had she come today to sell her vegetables? Or because she'd seen Daddy leave, and wanted to know what we had left in the house? I hoped Mama wouldn't tell her about the flour in the cellar. She could be a spy for Lee.

Then she came right out with it. "What are you going to do with that silver tea service, Leigh? You can't keep it here."

"I don't know yet," Mama said.

"It'd be the first thing the soldiers would take when they come to the house. And they'll be coming, Leigh. I heard they're all lean and hungry as wolves. They'll be begging for food at the door. Or at least for water."

"I don't know," Mama said again. And for a moment all three of us looked at the tea set. It sparkled as the afternoon sun slanted in the windows.

"Tell you what," Aunt Charlotte suggested. "You put it in a big basket and throw some old laundry over it, and I'll take it to my house for you. They'll soon find out I'm one of them. They won't take it from me."

I saw just a flicker of confusion in Mama's eyes.

Aunt Charlotte saw it, too. She reached across the table and put her hand, rough from working in her gardens, over Mama's. "You can trust me, Leigh," she said.

Mama nodded. "I know."

"Mama!" My voice didn't work right, I was so taken with surprise. "Mama, you can't!"

"And why can't I, Amelia?"

Did she want me to say it right out? The woman

was a Rebel, was why. She was lying! She'd likely turn it right over to the soldiers when they came. Or sell it. But all my training from Mama bade me hold my tongue. You didn't question the honesty of a friend. This was a friend, a neighbor, a business associate from town. Her word was good. Before the war, it had always worked that way here. Men shook hands on business arrangements in the street, and alliances were made for life.

Before the war.

Now what? I said nothing.

Mama stood up. "Go get the basket that holds my wash. It's in the yard, Amelia. I'll get the soiled clothes."

I did so. And the precious tea set that Mama's great-grandmother had saved on that long ride from Maine to Boston, throwing out all her clothing instead, was put in the basket, covered with soiled clothes. With a heaviness inside me, I walked it out to Aunt Charlotte's wagon where she set it in and proceeded to show us the best vegetables of the day. Mama selected some and paid her. They hugged, and Aunt Charlotte was on her way.

"Mama," I turned to her as the wagon went out into the street. "How could you?"

She smiled. "How could I, Amelia? She's a friend. I do hope things haven't come to such a pass that we stop trusting old friends because of this fracas going on."

"Mama, it's more than a fracas. Daddy says it's a civil war."

"Do you know what a civil war is, Amelia? A war that turns brother against brother, or sister against sister. It only becomes that when we allow it to be. So I shall call it a fracas. I know she's a Rebel. But so is Josh Dechart, isn't he?"

I had nothing to say to that. So I unhitched Pillow and mounted her. "If you don't see your tea set again, don't blame me," I mumbled, riding off. I was convinced of it.

The first thing that struck me about the Beale place was the silence. Not a living thing bestirred in the afternoon heat. Nothing, from the trees surrounding the neat white clapboard house to the fenced-in area around the barn.

Where was Patches, the dog? I knew he was old, but he never let a visitor approach without raising a fuss. Where were the horses? I dismounted at the gate and walked Pillow toward the house. The Beale farm was kept in wheat and corn. Some sheep grazed on a distant hill. They kept thirty acres in timber. South Mountain, just beyond the woods, was blue with September shadows and hovered over them menacingly this afternoon. From somewhere some crows called. But that was the only sound, and it was downright eerie.

"Jinny Pearl?" I tied Pillow to a fence post. "Mrs. Beale?"

No answer. I walked over to the barn and looked inside. The cows were munching hay. They raised their heads and gazed at me thoughtfully, then went back to eating. It would be milking time soon.

Then I heard it, the sound of digging. And soft voices carrying on the air. I went outside and around the back of the barn. Here the ground sloped down toward a stream, a runoff from Antietam Creek. And there in the distance I saw Jinny and her mother covering over something. I knew they had no silver tea service to bury, but people were hiding all kinds of things these days. I waved, thinking little of it.

Patches saw me and barked, and Jinny hushed him.

I waited while they finished their work. Then they walked up the slope toward me.

"Hello, Mrs. Beale."

She scarce looked at me. Just nodded, dropped her gaze to her hands, which she was wiping in her apron. "Cows have to be milked, Jinny," she called over her shoulder.

I saw blood on the apron. New blood.

Something was terribly wrong! Whose blood was

this? Why were they both so calm? Why did Jinny have to milk the cows? They'd hired a hand when Pruitt and Hiram, her brothers, left for the war. Why wasn't the hand here today?

Jinny had a shovel in one hand. Her bonnet was off, hanging down her back. She was a sturdy girl, but pretty, with unruly reddish brown hair that she wore in one braid down her back. It wasn't hard to see why Wes was taken with her. But now wisps of hair stuck out all over her forehead. The hem of her skirt and her apron were all covered with dirt. And blood. Jinny had blood on her, too.

"Hey, Amelia."

"Hey, Jinny."

"You should have given us notice that you were here."

"I called out. Nobody answered."

"Wes send you?"

"No. My daddy and Aunt Lou left this afternoon."

"Lucky them."

"Mama wants to know if you'd come by days and help with the housework. Until she can get somebody else. She'll pay two dollars a week and meals."

Her mother had gone into the house. Jinny and I walked to the barn, where we stood in the doorway, straw around our feet. A gray cat came over and rubbed my legs, then turned on its back and wiggled.

There was blood on Jinny's shoes, too. She took off her apron, hung it on a rung just inside the barn door, took down a clean one, and walked over to the pump, where she commenced to wash her hands and face. I followed and stood watching. She pumped with one hand and put her whole head under the water.

"You could stay for supper each night," I offered. "That way you'd see more of Wes. I don't think he's going back to St. James."

"Why should he? What good's school now? The whole world's gone crazy. Long as you can shoot a gun, that's all you need to know." She threw her hair back and wiped her face and neck with a piece of flannel. "Don't know as I want to see more of Wes now." Something about her frightened me.

"I know you two are fussing. Wes said so. But he didn't say why."

"We have our reasons."

"I hope that won't keep you from coming and helping. Mama would admire for you to come."

"There's so much work here now."

"Where's the hired man? Where's your pa?"

She continued drying herself. "In hiding."

"Your pa?" I looked around. Again the silence of the place struck me. It was ominous.

"He's hiding in the mountain. With the horses."

"What's he done?"

"Been reported as a solid Union man. Same as your pa. Only difference is he sometimes ventures down as far as that stone wall over yonder." She pointed to the wall, on the other side of the stream. "I bring his supper to him. Leave it on the wall. His breakfast, too."

"Does your mama suspect the hired man of informing? Is that why he isn't here?"

"No, he's sick. It's because of what happened this morning is why."

"What happened this morning?" I felt some terrible truth coming at me, like a runaway train.

"We hid all our things this morning," she said. "Ma's pewter plates are lowered into this well. I was going to the smokehouse to get some hams. That's when I saw him coming."

"Who?"

"A Rebel picket. A straggler from Jackson's army at Frederick. He said he was hungry and tired from the march up from Virginia, and the people of Maryland aren't welcoming them, like Lee thought. Said he was tired of it all already and would I give him something to eat."

I waited. She screwed up her pretty face, remembering.

"He was a straggler, is all. He told me Lee's split his army four ways. Said the Federals are fast coming and he wasn't about to be killed for Lee's stupidity. A general doesn't ever split his army. You know that, don't you. Everybody does. Joan of Arc knew it."

I didn't know it. And that she chose to lecture me on it now annoyed me. I wished she would get on with it. "What happened with the picket?" I pushed.

She sighed. "I had my arms full of ham. He made a nuisance of himself. I offered him a ham if he would go. He didn't want a ham."

"What did he want?"

"Me."

"Oh." The full force of it hit me between the eyes. "Oh," I said again.

"Stupid me. I'd left my revolver in the barn."

"So what did you do?"

"I sweet-talked him. All the way back to the barn. I put down the smoked hams and sweet-talked him some more, so he didn't see me pick up my pistol. I hid it under my apron. I led him toward the hayloft. Then I shot him dead."

I didn't know what to say. She had killed somebody. Shot him dead. The finality of it fell over me like a shroud. She was only three years older than I was, and she had killed a man.

At that moment the fact of the war came home to me. It had nothing to do with Mama's tea set, the flour we had stored in our cellar, or even with my daddy having to leave. It had to do with a young girl coming out of her mama's smokehouse on a peaceful farm and having to shoot a Rebel straggler because he made unseemly advances toward her.

This was worse than my causing Mr. Dechart's newspaper to be wrecked. Jinny Pearl had killed somebody! Worse yet, she was so calm about it. Of course, her idol was Joan of Arc. But Joan of Arc was in a book.

Some line had been crossed today. And I think Jinny knew it.

"You can't tell anybody," she said. "Ma said not to tell anybody. He'll never be missed, Ma said. And if he is, the Rebs will consider him a deserter. Especially, you can't tell Wes."

"Don't you think he'd want to know?"

"He'd find fault. He doesn't like a lot of what I'm about these days."

What was she about these days? What had Wes been talking about? Something, something here, even more than the dead soldier, if there could be more. But I couldn't get a purchase on it.

"Unless you promise not to tell Wes, I won't come and help your mother."

I nodded. What did I care about my stupid brother. She'd confided in me, not him. Then a thought came to me.

"Why did you tell me, Jinny? You didn't have to."

She laughed and looked down at herself. "All this blood?"

"You could have killed some chickens."

Her face grew solemn. "I had to tell somebody. I always liked you, Amelia. Especially after what you did after Dewitt got shot. You did something right."

"I don't feel so good about that, Jinny."

"Doing right doesn't always make you feel good. I don't care what they tell you in church."

"I don't know what Wes ever told you about me, but after what happened to Josh's father, I've resolved to stay out of this war."

She shrugged. "I think you're wrong in your resolve. But that's out of the whole cloth now. You'll find, soon enough, that you can't stay out. You'll have to commit yourself, sooner or later, one way or another. Being a woman doesn't get you out of it."

"Will you come, then, and help Mama?"

"Be proud to," she said.

CHAPTER FIVE

By the Dawn's Early Light

The next day two things happened. General Lee came through town. Just marched right through with his men and horse-drawn ambulances full of sick soldiers, pretty as you please.

And Jinny Pearl came to help my mama.

Before first light I awoke to the smells of bacon cooking downstairs. And coffee. Coffee! Where'd it come from? Coffee and tea were so dear that we'd all but given up both this year. Mama had a small reserve set aside for when company came, the last of what Daddy had had in the store. Mama said she lost her elasticity of spirit without her coffee.

The smell of it drew me right downstairs, into the kitchen where Jinny Pearl was bent over the black stove.

"Good morning!" she said. She looked right perky, all done up in a fresh calico skirt, homespun blouse, and crisp apron. I began to think I'd dreamed it all up about the killing.

"Coffee! Where'd it come from?"

She turned from the stove, smiling. "My mama sent it."

"How nice you look, Jinny," I said. Her hair hung in a neat braid down her back. It even had a ribbon on the end of it.

The kitchen door opened, and Wes came in with a basket of eggs. He scarce looked at Jinny Pearl. Just set the basket down on the counter.

"Oh, brown eggs. I love brown eggs!" Jinny exclaimed. "Thank you."

"They don't taste any different from white ones." Wes sat down at the table and poured himself some coffee. I saw the hurt look on Jinny's face and kicked him under the table, but he paid me no mind. He needed some elasticity of spirit. Having Jinny in the house wasn't going to work if Wes didn't behave.

I set the table for breakfast, the way I used to for Aunt Lou. Jinny had biscuits in the oven. "Where's Mama?" I asked.

"With your little brother," Jinny answered, "putting buckets of water out front."

"What for?"

Jinny turned to me. "For the soldiers." Her face was grim.

"The Rebel soldiers?"

She checked the biscuits. "She says our heavenly Father said we should give water even to our enemies." I could not see Jinny's face, but I knew she was thinking of the Reb soldier buried on their farm. Quickly I went through the hallway and out the front door. Sure enough, there was Sky, lugging a bucket of water to the front gate. Mama was setting down another.

I went to her. "Mama, you shouldn't be doing this."

"And why not? Our heavenly Father says to."

"Mama, I know scripture, too, and I don't ever remember anything about giving water to Rebel soldiers."

"You are splitting hairs, Amelia. Now go in and help Jinny. I didn't ask you to help me, did I? I could see your objection if I did, but I didn't."

Sky was in a state of feverish excitement. "They're coming to town. Today. I heard they got a hundred and four pieces of cannon. Four, twelve, and eighteen pounders! And I heard they have a pet cow they brought all the way from Richmond!"

"Come, let's all go and have breakfast," Mama said.

"Aw, do I have to? I wanna wait here for the army. Suppose I miss 'em?"

"I don't think we'll miss them, Sky, come on, now. I must say, Amelia, Jinny Pearl is wonderful. She was here, starting the stove, before I was up this morning."

"She brought coffee," I said.

"I know. I'll have to fix something for her to take back to her mother when she goes home tonight. If it'll be safe for her to go home. I do worry, what with the army coming through."

Jinny can manage an army, I thought. No need to worry. "Wes is not being nice to her, Mama. I know you don't like tales out of school, but I feel sorry for Jinny."

She sighed. "I don't know what's going on between those two. But I think Jinny can hold her own and we should leave them be. Unless Wes gets outright rude."

Jinny wouldn't set and eat with us, though Mama invited her to. "We'd be proud to have you join us, Jinny."

No. She'd eat later. She would go directly upstairs and air out the bed linens. Wes sat sulkily, spooning his food into his mouth.

"Your father is paying her, Wes," Mama reminded him. "You could at least be civil. I have need of her services."

He did not reply.

"If not for her sake, then for mine. I didn't raise you to be boorish. Now, I need you to secure the gate to the hen coop. Word is there will be some robbing of hens before this day is over. And put the horses in the barn. I understand horses are going to be in dire demand by the soldiers, too. Then you might ride over to the college and see if anyone is reporting for class."

"Not going back to college," he said.

Mama sipped her coffee carefully. She wasn't pretty, my mama. Her hair was like old straw, after harvest. Her complexion was good, but she was plain. It was her nose that saved her face. It had sort of a squared-off tip that made you stare at it. Then your gaze went to her eyes, which were blue and very intelligent. Then you started to notice how the plainness added up to something more than pretty. Interesting was more the word.

"You are going back, Wes," she said. "Your father has paid your tuition and board. He wants you to have this education. A young man needs all the education he can get these days."

Wes hunched his shoulders. He was fair-haired like Mama, but he had Daddy's dark eyes and long, narrow face, which was just acquiring the hard planes of a man. "Kyd Douglas studied law at Franklin and Marshall, and what was it for? He's on Stonewall Jackson's staff now."

"Well there, you see?" Mama said brightly. "I'll wager he wouldn't have such a position if he hadn't gone to college!"

Wes was saying something about never hearing such fool logic, something he wouldn't have said if Daddy was there, when we heard the sound. Fifes and drums. The sound of "Dixie." The rumble of wagons, the shouts of soldiers, and barks of a command.

"They're here!" Like a shot, Sky was out of his seat, through the hall, and out the front door.

Wes reached for his rifle in the corner. When he turned he had a different look. Alert, determined. He even appeared taller.

"No, Wes," Mama said. "Put it down."

"Nobody'll take our chickens." His face was white, set. "I'm man of the house, with Pa gone. I have to give a good account of myself."

"Then use discretion and don't endanger us," Mama told him.

Slowly, he put the rifle down and we went outside.

"Look at the cannons!" Sky yelled. "Look at them!"

Wes dragged behind Mama and Sky, and I dragged with him. "You're being absolutely nasty to

Mama," I whispered savagely. "Can't you see how hard it is for her with Daddy gone?"

"Mind your own business."

"It is my business. What's wrong with you, anyway? Jinny is being so gracious. Can't you at least meet her halfway?"

"You don't know anything about Jinny," he growled.

What more was there to know than that she'd killed a Rebel soldier? And he didn't know that! What was he talking about? I pinched him and ran to catch up with Mama at the gate.

All our neighbors were standing at their gates, watching the army go by. So many of them! Hundreds of soldiers, tramp, tramp, tramping. Some grinned at us. Some raised their hats and nodded hello. And, like Aunt Charlotte had said, they seemed a seedy lot, not at all dashing and well turned out, as we'd been told the Confederates were. And if what they wore could pass as uniforms, well then, I would say the Union army was much better equipped.

All in all, they were a rough-looking lot. They looked like outriders, like vagrants. Was this what the Rebel picket Jinny had shot had looked like? Their eyes were red-rimmed. Some were coughing. And their officers were not much better. You could scarce tell them apart from the men, except that they wore neater uniforms of a sort of gray color, some with small stars on their collars. Or bars, depending on their rank. And because they had good boots on their feet and they rode horses.

"Oh, dear," I heard Mama moan. I looked up at her and she pointed. "Ambulances, look, and the men are all ill."

The ambulances rumbled by, raising even more dust than the men on foot. There were a lot of ambulances. "We will have sickness again," Mama predicted.

Some of the ambulances had "United States" painted on the side.

"Stolen, likely," Wes murmured, "stolen in some battle in Virginia." There was pure disdain in his voice.

We watched as the cannon, wagons, and ambulances rumbled by. Then we heard a neighbor cry, "There's General Lee!"

Sure enough, there he was, riding in front of one of the common ambulances, with a Palmetto flag flying over it, his arm in a sling. He sat up there like some elegant gentleman would sit in his own parlor. Six officers on horseback, heavily armed, hovered about the wagon. Lee lifted his hat and waved.

His hair was pure white. His eyes the bluest of blue. And as he rode by, Sky called out, "General Lee!

General Lee!" He looked in our direction, waved, and smiled. And I just know he waved right at me.

Some of our neighbors were cheering him. Others booed. Then, of a sudden, there was a commotion. A woman had run out into the street and was singing "The Star-Spangled Banner." Her voice rose over the din of wagon wheels, horses' hooves, and marching feet.

She ran right up to Lee, past the officers on horseback, and the sweet words of the song stopped the whole parade.

One of Lee's protectors started off his horse to stop her.

"No," Lee ordered, "let her finish."

It all happened so fast and in such confusion that I never noticed who it was. Sky did. "It's Jinny Pearl," he said. "Listen."

The world came to a standstill as Jinny Pearl stood there in her calico skirt, homespun blouse, and apron, and finished her song. *And the rockets' red glare, the bombs bursting in air, gave proof through the night, that our flag was still there. Oh, say does that star-spangled banner yet wave? O'er the land of the free. And the home of the brave.*

Beside me, I felt Wes move as if to go to her. But Mama's hand stayed him. "Leave her be," she whispered. "She has to do this." So Wes stood still.

A shiver ran through me. I looked at Mama and saw tears in her eyes.

Jinny Pearl finished and stood, clutching her apron in her hands and looking up at Lee. Silence, terrible silence then, while we held our breaths. All that could be heard was a cough or two, a murmur from some neighbors, and the rattle of some horses' bridles.

Lee lifted his hat and looked down at Jinny Pearl. His officers were off their horses now, ready to move her. "Stand back," Lee ordered softly. Then to Jinny Pearl. "Miss, I am honored," he said. "And I promise, the people of Maryland will not suffer in any way from this invasion."

I held my breath, hoping Jinny wouldn't take it in her head to tell him how she had already suffered from the invasion. Whatever she said, it was murmured to him, and I know it wasn't about the picket she killed, because Lee's face stayed soft. "The boys are rather hungry, however," he amended. "And there may be some robbing of hen coops. But I promise there will be no serious plunder."

Then everything started up again and they moved on. More supply wagons and ambulances. And there was a pet cow with a ribbon on her halter, her bell clanging as she walked along. And cattle, lots of them, following.

After Lee passed, two soldiers, having seen our

water buckets, dropped out of line. "Could we have some of that water, ma'am?" The Southern accents were thick.

"Of course," Mama said. She nodded to Sky, who'd been just waiting for this, and he dipped the ladle into the buckets, handing it to one of them.

But before the man took it, he looked at Mama. "You Secesh, ma'am? Or Yankee?"

"For the Union," Mama said firmly.

He grinned. "Boys," he called out to some others who were coming over, "this lady is a Yankee." Then he turned to me. "Would you drink the water first, miss?"

I stared. "Why?"

But Mama knew. "It isn't poisoned," she said. Her voice had a note of weariness in it. "Drink it, Amelia."

I took a sip from the ladle. The soldier tipped his hat. "Much obliged, miss." Then he drank and passed the ladle to his comrades.

Four or five of them drank before an officer rode up. "A Yankee lady is giving out water?" he asked.

"Yes, sir. Good and cold, too," one of them said.

Sky offered him a fresh ladle full, holding it up.

The officer was young and well-turned out, with a saber and a mustard-colored sash around his waist. His horse was handsome and well-groomed, his coat as shiny as a polished nut. The officer took the ladle from Sky, held it a moment, then dashed it to the ground. "I won't drink a drop of Yankee water," he said. Then he put the spurs to his horse, turned it, and rode away.

Sky picked up the ladle. His round, freckled face was all pinched up, fighting tears. Wes started forward, fists clenched. Only a tight grip from Mama's hand on his arm stayed him.

"It's all right, Wes. It's only water. The others were grateful."

Wes couldn't seem to contain himself. He was breathing heavily and glaring. "Some of them are even younger than me," he growled.

Some other men who had already accepted the water seemed abashed. Then the one who had first come up to us took off his battered hat and spoke for all the rest. "Powerful sorry, ma'am. Son." He looked at Wes. "Don't take no offense. He's been drinkin' somethin' more than water. And he's spent. Hope you don't think the rest of us ain't beholden. 'Cause we are."

"No problem, soldier. No offense taken," Mama returned. "Now you'd best return to your ranks or you'll get into trouble. Come, children, let's go back inside."

We walked back to the house. Wes lingered.

"Leave it be, Wes," Mama said, "please."

But he was looking at Jinny now, who was still standing in the street. "She still thinks she's Joan of Arc," he mumbled. He went out the gate, walking toward her slowly.

"Mama!" I said.

"Let them solve their own problems." She turned us to the house. I didn't know about Mama, but I felt drained, as if hours had passed in those last twenty minutes or so. It had been so wearing, what with the drama of seeing all those men, laying eyes upon the famous Lee, and then Jinny Pearl running out there like that.

"Wasn't Lee fine?" Sky asked.

"Oh, yes, he looked like a real fine gentleman," Mama answered.

"Wasn't Jinny Pearl wonderful?" I asked.

"She was brave," Mama agreed. "The girl does have pluck."

You don't know the half of it, I thought. Before we went in the front door I turned to look. Jinny and Wes on the side of the street. Arguing.

CHAPTER SIX

Gentlemen Callers

SEPTEMBER 12, 1862

The next morning, Jinny Pearl would not tell me what she had said to General Lee. "No matter," she said.

"But he's a general! And famous! You could have told him anything you wanted!"

"I did. But that's between me and General Lee."

Her and General Lee? Jinny Pearl Beale, who still wore homespun? It made me mad, her having airs like that. Oh, she didn't simper like Lutie Kealhofer. But airs were airs, whether they wore silk or homespun.

"Now, you going to set the table for breakfast or not?" she asked.

She was bossy, too. This was my daddy's house, my mama's kitchen, yet when she was working in it, I felt beholden just to be allowed to help her. I'd gotten up before Mama to help her this morning. Wes wasn't anywhere to be found. Kindling had to be brought in for the stove, eggs from the henhouse. I'd done both.

Why is it that people who are the most ornery to us can make us feel downright happy when they favor us with a nice word? Why do they hold such sway over us? I set the table.

"Joan of Arc couldn't have done any better than you did yesterday," I told her.

"Joan of Arc's nothing," she said. "It's that Belle Boyd I'd like to meet someday."

"Who's Belle Boyd?" I felt stupid, like I should know more. I hated feeling like that, and it humbled me. I hated, even more, feeling humbled.

"The woman Rebel spy."

My eyes widened. "A Rebel? And you want to meet her?"

"I met Lee, didn't I? The first thing you have to learn in times of war is to know and respect your enemy. If you don't, you're a fool. I'd like to talk to Belle Boyd. She may be a Rebel, but she stands up for what she believes in. And she doesn't let being a woman keep her from doing things."

I set down the linen napkins beside each plate. "What did she do?"

"Last May. Front Royal, when Jackson attacked.

She found out that Front Royal was going to be abandoned by the Yankees and all their stores would be left. She ran past Yankee lines to tell Jackson. She also told him where the Federal guns were. She did this at her own risk. She was shot at, and when Jackson offered her a horse and an escort away from the fighting, she said no. She said the men needed their horses. Now, who says women can't do important things in this war?"

"Is she like Joan of Arc?"

She scoffed. "I don't care about her anymore."

"Why?"

She looked at me as if I was dim-witted. "Books. I got her from books. Real life isn't like that. After you kill a Rebel picket, you don't need heroines from books anymore. What was it like in France when Joan of Arc was leading her army? It's just as bad here now. And there's things that need to be done. Why can't women do them?"

"You already have," I said.

"That's just it. Now I know I can do more."

"You want to be a spy, then?"

"Don't know yet. But I'll know when the time comes."

Mama and Sky came into the kitchen for breakfast. Then Wes. We sat down to eat. Jinny started the makings for a pie at a table in the corner.

"Lee's made his headquarters in a grove just outside town," Wes said.

"So you were out in the streets, then," Mama said, "when you were supposed to be doing morning chores. Amelia had to do them."

"It won't kill her," Wes said.

"That isn't the point, Wes."

"What is the point, then?" He stared across the table at Mama.

For a moment it looked as if she had lost her elasticity of spirit. Then she got it right back again. "That as man of the house, with your father gone, you should see to some of these chores."

"As man of the house, I should be allowed to sit in Pa's chair," Wes retorted.

"I just can't bear to have anyone sit in your father's chair," Mama said. "He's coming back. It's a sign of respect that we hold his place for him, Wes."

Wes dismissed the thought. "The town is full of Confederates," he said. "I thought someone should go and get some intelligence about things. All the houses are shuttered. The stores all have 'sold out' signs on the windows. Nobody's open."

"Did you go past the *Hagerstown Mail*?" I asked. "Has anybody written 'traitor' in paint on the front windows?"

Wes looked at me. "Why would anyone do that now, with the Confederates in town?"

I shrugged and didn't answer. So, Josh was all right, then. He didn't need me.

"The Confederates are lounging around like they own the place," Wes retorted. "But they didn't bother me and my friends when we walked on the sidewalks."

"Your friends?" Mama asked. "What friends?"

Wes didn't answer. "Everybody says there's gonna be a battle. Right here in town."

"Whoopee!" from Sky.

"Nonsense," from Mama. "They wouldn't fight in town. You heard what Lee told Jinny Pearl last evening. The people won't suffer from this invasion."

"You believe that, Mama, and you're more gullible than I thought," Wes told her.

I saw Jinny fling a look at Wes. A disgusted look. And I thought, these two are so full of feeling that if someone lit a candle right now, the whole room would blow up. Together, they are like a loaded weapon. She is powder, he is shot.

Just about then there came a rapping at the back door. We all sat looking at each other.

"I'll go." Wes started to push back his chair.

"No!" Mama put her hand on his arm. "Jinny Pearl will answer it."

I saw the look on Wes's face then. Pure hatred it was, directed at Mama. You shouldn't have done that, Mama, I thought, but of course I didn't say it.

Jinny Pearl opened the door.

Three men stood there. Two were Rebel officers. The other was Mr. Hanson Beachley. He was Daddy's head clerk at the store, a ninny if there ever was one. He never wanted to take responsibility for anything. If you went to the store and asked him for something, a piece of candy, for instance, he'd say, ask your father; I don't want to be responsible.

What was a head clerk for, if not to be responsible? He was the reason Daddy had left the store keys with Mama. Why did Daddy keep him, I'd once asked Mama. "He has a good head for sums," she said.

Right now he didn't look like it. He looked like if you asked him how many Rebel officers were standing with him, he'd say Lee's whole army. He looked terrified.

"I hate to disturb you all at breakfast," he said.

"Yes, Mr. Beachley." Mama stood up. "Do come in, please."

He came into the kitchen, the two Rebel officers with him. They were a sorry looking pair. Their uniforms were dusty, their boots worn, their moustaches needed trimming. But they were polite enough as they stood there, with their dog-eared hats in their hands. I saw their eyes go over the table with all the food. And for one crazy moment, I felt bad for them. I wondered how long it had been since they'd been in a kitchen, and had home-cooking.

"These gentlemen came to me," Mr. Beachley said. "They would like the keys to the store."

Wes opened his mouth to object, but Mama spoke first. "The store is closed, gentlemen."

"There's no sign on it, ma'am," one of the officers said. He must have been the senior officer, because he had small stars on his collar. And I recollected that Josh had told me that officers of lesser rank had silver bars.

"All the other stores have signs that say 'sold out,' ma'am," he said in a honey-like drawl, "though I just can't figure who bought them out all of a sudden."

"We put up no sign, but there is little left in our store," Mama told him.

"Whatever little there is, is more than we have now to dress up our rations," the senior officer said.

Silence for a moment. I saw Mama's indecision.

"They'll pay in Confederate money," Mr. Beachley told her. "And from what I understand, it's good as gold."

"That's not what I heard," Wes put in.

The two officers turned to look at Wes, who had his chair pushed back from the table and was lounging with his coffee cup in his hand. "Son," said the senior officer, "I don't reckon I was speaking to you."

"Well, I'm speaking to you," Wes retorted.

"Son," came the same soft drawl, "don't get mouthy. I just can't stand it when young people get mouthy."

"Wes, be still," Mama ordered.

Wes got red in the face. The officer turned again to Mama. "Ma'am, we mean to pay for anything we take. But if you refuse, why, I just can't be responsible for the actions of our men."

Mama took a deep breath and smiled. "Well, then, I might as well give over the keys, mightn't I?"

"Yes, ma'am." And the officer gave a little bow.

"I'll fetch them," Mama said. And she started out of the room.

"Mama, you can't!" Wes protested. He stood up.

At the door to the hallway, Mama stopped and turned. "Yes, I can, Wes. You heard what this gentleman said. You wouldn't want the store broken into, now, would you? Besides, your father left the keys in my care. So the decision is mine to make."

Wes slammed down his cup so hard I thought it would break. Then he strode out of the room, pushing right past Mama. I heard his boots clomping up the stairs.

Mama smiled. "Forgive my son, gentlemen. You

know how hasty young people are these days. All taken with the spirit of things. I have all I can do to keep him from running off to war."

"Don't let him go, ma'am, if you can help it," the senior officer advised.

Mama smiled. "Jinny Pearl, why don't you fetch these men a hot cup of coffee and some biscuits, while I get the keys." And she went down the hall.

There was a moment of terrible silence and embarrassment. Nobody knew what to do. Except Sky.

"Why don't y'all come and set?" he invited. He stood up and pulled out chairs.

Mr. Beachley came first. The others followed and sat down gingerly.

I jumped up to get clean cups. For a moment I had a terrible thought. Would Jinny be able to serve them, after what had happened at her farm with the Rebel picket? But I needn't have feared. Jinny was in charge of herself. She not only served coffee, she brought over a fresh plate of biscuits. They thanked her and commenced to eat.

Sky was openmouthed as the senior officer sat down next to him. He stared up at the man. "You do any fightin'?" he asked.

"Yes, son. I have."

"You kill anybody?"

"Hush, Sky," I ordered sharply.

"S'all right, miss," the senior officer said, "I got a young 'un at home. He's the same way." Then to Sky. "Yes, son, I think I have killed people. But I'm not proud of it."

"Then why you fightin'?" Sky persisted.

"Because I have to," came the reply.

"Well, I wish I could fight. I'd kill. And I wouldn't be sorry for it. Not a bit. Nosir."

The man set his mug down carefully. "Be glad you're too young, son," he said. Then he thanked Jinny for the coffee.

For a few moments, the five of us sat at our kitchen table — me and Sky, Mr. Beachley and the two officers. I thought how out of place they looked here in our kitchen, with their dusty uniforms and swords and their mustard-colored gloves tucked into their sashes. Then, of a sudden, the junior officer must have recognized Jinny.

"Aren't you the little gal who was singing to General Lee yesterday?" he asked.

Jinny straightened up from where she'd been bending over the oven to check the pie. "No," she said, "I'm the woman who sang to General Lee."

"Well, I'll be dad-blamed," the man said. "That was a right gutsy thing to do, miss, if you don't mind me saying so."

"I don't mind," Jinny said cooly. But she turned to

do some other chore, not giving him the satisfaction of seeing his praise had pleased her.

Silence, then, until Mama returned. "Gentlemen, here are the keys to the store. I would appreciate it if they were returned to me when you are finished. And if an accounting is given to me, also."

"Everything will be in order, ma'am," the senior officer said. He pocketed the keys, took a final sip of coffee, and stood up, looking longingly at the two remaining biscuits on the plate.

"Take them," Mama said.

"Thank you, ma'am. Much obliged."

They all walked to the door. There the senior officer turned. "I must say, ma'am, it's been a pleasure being in a real home, if only for a few minutes. And I must commend your common sense, in giving us the keys."

Mama stood, proud and erect. "My husband left the decision to me," she said.

The man bowed. "Honored to make your acquaintance," he said.

In the next moment, they were all gone. And we stood staring at one another in the kitchen, as if they had never come. As if we had dreamed it.

Mama sank down in her chair at the table. I saw that her face was white, that her hands were shaking. "Dear God, I hope I did the right thing," she said.

"You did right," Jinny said. "Here, let me fix you a cup of fresh coffee."

Mama took it with still-shaking hands. "Thank you, Jinny, you've turned out to be a real comfort. And you two" — she looked at me and Sky — "behaved very well. I'm proud of you. But I feel bad about Wes. I know he doesn't approve of my giving them the keys."

"That isn't why he's spoiling for a fight," Jinny said.

"Why, then?" Mama stared at her.

But Jinny only smiled. "You did the right thing, Mrs. Grafton," she said again. "It wasn't the time to stand up to the Rebels. When the time comes, you'll know it."

Her words gratified Mama. But they sent a chill through me.

CHAPTER SEVEN

Isn't There More to It Than That?

The tramping of feet out in the street pulled me from sleep the next morning while the light outside was still gray. It was Saturday, September thirteenth. I remember the date because I was so glad the thirteenth didn't fall on Friday that year. When it does, you have to be careful of black cats crossing your path, walking under ladders, and having hooty owls call outside your window. More soldiers, I thought, as my eyes flew open. More soldiers for Lee. Then I thought, I'll take black cats, hooty owls, and ladders, any day. Then I heard another sound. Someone was creeping down the stairs. I got out of bed and put on my robe.

It was Wes. I knew it as sure as I knew that my middle name was Francine, a name I didn't go out of my way to mention if I didn't have to. I went into the hall and peered over the bannister.

It was Wes. He was moving about quietly in the rooms below. I heard Duke and Duchess moving about, too, heard their soft whining, heard him hush them. I crept downstairs.

He was in the kitchen, wrapping some leftover biscuits in a napkin, stuffing them in some kind of sack he wore slung from his shoulder. He was dressed for leaving.

He was running off to join the army.

I couldn't stand it. My world was falling apart. Daddy was gone, Jinny Pearl had killed a Rebel soldier, and now my brother was going off to war. Wes looked the part already. He had a rolled-up blanket tied on his back like all the soldiers who'd ever passed through town, Rebel or Yankee. And his musket was set down beside him, leaning against the stove. "Wes," I whispered.

He turned, saw me. "Can you get some ham and slice it for me?"

I went to the larder where the ham was kept. I brought it out, somehow found a knife, and set these things on the table. "Wes, you can't," I said.

"Why can't I?"

"You'll break Mama's heart."

"I'll break my own if I have to stay around here anymore."

"Don't you care about Mama?"

He didn't answer.

"Well," I said, "if you want to go off and get yourself killed then go ahead. See if I care."

"You going to slice the ham for me? Or do I have to do it?"

I sliced several pieces for him and almost sliced off a finger twice. He took another napkin and wrapped the ham in it and stuffed that into the sack, too.

"What is that thing you're wearing?" I asked.

"A haversack. Mrs. Jones made it for me."

"You're running off with the Jones boys, then."

He gave me a level stare. "Where have you been, Amelia? Open your eyes, see what's going on around here."

I didn't want to open my eyes. I'd seen enough in the last few days to last me forever.

"Almost everybody in town my age has gone for a soldier. Do you think I want to sit around here and have Mama tell me to behave? To not talk back to the Rebels? To collect the eggs from the henhouse? She won't even let me sit in Pa's chair."

"Would that keep you from going?" I asked. "If she let you sit in Daddy's chair?"

He made a scoffing sound in his throat. "Stop being a girl," he said.

"What else am I supposed to be, Wes?"

"I know you can't help it. Any more than Jinny can."

"Is it on account of Jinny? Is that why you're going? Because you've had an argument? Or to show her how brave you are?"

He glared at me.

The thought came over me then like a warm blanket. "Wes, I know Jinny's all fired up about things. And I know you're mad 'cause of what she did with General Lee the other day, but you don't have to run off and join the army to show her you're brave."

He picked up his musket. "You don't know anything about Jinny," he said. "For your information, it has to do with her, yes. In part. But not how you think."

"How, then?"

"You wouldn't believe if I told you."

Did he know about the Rebel soldier, then? No, I was sure of it. Then what did he know about Jinny that I didn't know? It scared me. But I knew there was something terrible just beneath the surface, with those two, something dark and swirling and threatening to pull them both in.

"I'm going," he said. "Now, you going to tell me good-bye or not?"

I stood staring at him. "Good-bye, Wes."

We stared at each other. He was my brother, and I supposed that I loved him, though most of the time we fussed at each other. Could he do this? Just pick up his musket, walk out of the kitchen with some ham in his haversack, and go to war? Wasn't there more to it than that? Tears came to my eyes. "I don't want you to go, Wes," I said.

"Walk me outside. The Jones boys will be here soon."

I followed him quietly out the back door and around the side of the house, and there, at the front gate, were the Jones boys. They both had blanket rolls and muskets, slouched hats, and haversacks.

"Howdy, Amelia," Travis said.

Sixteen, he was. Cole was fifteen. "They'll never take you," I told them.

Travis grinned. "It's all set. We've signed on."

Cole nodded, then looked at my brother. "She gonna run right inside and tell yer ma?"

"Are you?" Wes looked at me.

Was I? I should. I knew I should. But I just stood rooted to the spot. "No," I said. "I won't tell."

"Well, let's be off, then." Wes looked at me sheepishly. "Look after Jinny," he said.

Look after Jinny? She wasn't the one who needed looking after.

"And tell her something for me. Tell her . . ." He hesitated, then spoke again. "Tell her, so there. I did it before her. Go and do it if she wants. See if I care. Tell her I hope she's happy now."

Whatever lay between them it was like a boil needing lancing. Oh Wes, I thought, you don't have to go to war over it. You don't have to get yourself killed! I reached out and hugged him. "Take care of yourself."

He hugged me back, with more fervor than I'd expected. "Tell Ma not to worry her head. I'll be fine."

Then they walked off. Like they were going to the drugstore for a soda.

When Wes didn't appear for breakfast, Mama thought he was sleeping late. Then she saw Jinny Pearl bringing in the eggs, and that got all her elasticity going.

She was already seated at the table. She threw down her napkin, got up, and started for the hall. "That boy!" she said.

"Mama!" I called out. But she paid me no mind. Just started right up the stairs. I sat at the table waiting. In a few minutes I heard her footsteps coming back down. She stood in the doorway of the kitchen.

"Wes is gone," she said.

I didn't say a word. "Gone where?" Both Jinny and Sky said it at the same time.

"His bed is all made up. His room is neat. You know the bowie knife your father gave him last Christmas? It's gone." Then she looked in the corner by the fireplace, and her shoulders drooped. "His musket is gone, too."

"Maybe he went back to college," said Sky.

"With his knife and gun? They wouldn't allow it on campus. My boy has gone for a soldier." Mama's hand went over her heart.

"Whoopee!" Sky yelled. "My brother is a soldier!"

"We must find him before he does this foolish thing." Mama took off her apron. "Jinny Pearl, what do you know of this?"

Jinny hesitated. Could she lie to Mama? But what truth did she know? "I always suspected, ma'am, that someday Wes was going to join the army," she said.

"Wes was angry with me for giving the keys. Is that it, Jinny?" Mama cut right to the chase.

"No, ma'am, but he was afraid."

"Afraid?" Mama laughed. "Wes was afraid of nothing, Jinny."

"He was afraid that he'd go and do something just awful with the Rebels in town. And get you all into trouble."

I had to admire Jinny. None of what she was feeling was showing in her face. She could be Miss Sly Boots, all right.

Mama sighed. "I just hope I didn't drive him to it."

"I'm sure you didn't," Jinny said. "I think maybe Wes just wanted to prove he was brave."

"Brave? Dear God in heaven!" Mama put her hands to cover her mouth and whirled around in confusion for a moment. Then she gathered herself in. "I must go and find him," she said. "Where do you think I should start?" She looked at us.

"Maybe he went with the Jones boys," I volunteered. No, I wasn't being disloyal to Wes. He and the Jones boys were likely out of Washington County by now. And it was the least I could do for Mama.

"Yes, of course. Amelia, can you hitch up the wagon?"

"I can," Sky said.

"No. You stay here, Sky. I need to post you as a lookout. In case Wes comes back. And if he does, you tell him I need him here and not to run off again, you hear me?"

Sky swelled with importance. I ran outside.

"What are you going to say to Mrs. Jones, Mama?"

"Say?" Mama adjusted her gloves. It was a fine September day, with just a hint of burnt color on the trees. The sun poured like liquid gold, the dappled shadows made by the trees were near-blue. Everything stood out like in a painting. I could see us as if from a distance, jogging along the dusty road in our little wagon. I wished we could be in a painting, that none of this was real. I wished we never had to get to the end of the road, to the mean little Jones farm on the edge of the woods and have that woman tell Mama the boys were long-since gone.

"Say? Well, I don't know. But I'm sure Travis and Cole put your brother up to this. That woman should be told."

"Told what, Mama?"

"Well, that she should have kept her boys away from mine, for one thing."

"Mama, you can't say that."

"Why can't I?"

"Because it sounds as if you don't think Travis and Cole are good enough for Wes."

"Well, of course that's not what I meant. But your father and I didn't send Wes to college to have him run off with some mountain boys."

It was what she meant, then. Did she know how she sounded? I hoped she wouldn't sound that way to Mrs. Jones.

"Now, just pull right up here by the front gate," she said. "We'll walk."

I hitched the horse to the gate post and looked around. Somehow the beautiful September day seemed to have vanished. Where had the sun gone? There was a brooding darkness to this place, sitting as it did in the shadow of the mountain. The house was a cabin, no more, made of chinked logs. I think they still had glazed paper on the windows, and some half-hearted smoke puffed out of the one chimney.

Mama lifted her skirts as we walked through the scrubby ground. "Likely they still sleep on corn husk mattresses." Mama wasn't an unkind person. She was the first in town to come to the aid of a poor family or start a collection at church for a new widow. But she was angry now.

"If Wes had to run off, why didn't he go with someone like Henry Kyd Douglas?" she asked.

"Because Douglas is a Rebel, Mama."

The distinction was lost on her as we made our way through the clutter that surrounded the cabin. Empty barrels, discarded mattresses, broken farm machinery, even an old rusty kettle lay strewn about in abandon. Scraggly chickens clucked around our feet. Behind the house, animal hides were nailed to the ground all over the place — squirrel, possum, rabbit, even fox.

"Mrs. Jones!" Mama called out. But nobody answered. The place seemed deserted.

"Let's go, Mama. She can't help us. There's nobody here."

"Yes, there is. Look yonder. There's somebody down by the creek."

There was a small creek down by the timberwood. Undaunted, Mama picked her way, and I followed. Why, even the soil is mean around here, I thought, scanning the fields. They looked worn out, the earth not rich and brown, like it was on the Beale farm, but soft and ashy, untrustworthy. How could they grow anything here? I wondered. And I knew the Joneses grew everything they ate.

The woman was doing the family laundry in the creek. She'd placed many articles of clothing on some rocks and the water was rushing over it. I smelled the lye soap, saw her reddened hands, and then, when she stood to greet us, saw she was as worn-down as the soil around her.

"Y'all lost your way?" she asked.

"No," Mama answered. "You're Mrs. Jones, aren't you? Isn't this the Jones farm?"

"If'n that's what you wanna call it. How kin I help ye?"

"I'm Mrs. Grafton. This is my daughter, Amelia."

Her eyes took us in. Our clothes, our un-red hands, the way Mama spoke, her lace mitts, everything. "Town folk," she said. There was no disdain in her voice. It was said sad-like, though. "What kin I do fer ye?"

"My boy Wes has run off this day to join the army," Mama told her. "And I'm afraid he's gone off with your boys. Are they missing?"

The woman stepped off the rock she was working on. She had bare feet. Her ragged dress was soaked around the edges. Her hair, secured back in a bun, was coming undone. Her face was burned by the sun, like she'd been working the fields.

"Gone as yesterday's rain," she said. "Crept out early this mornin'. I heard 'em go. Didn't even get off my mattress. T'weren't nuthin' I could do to stop 'em, and wasn't worth the try."

"Gone where?" Mama asked.

"To the army," the woman said patiently. "Likely halfway to Washington City by now. Said somethin' yesterday 'bout the Potomac Home Brigade. Infantry. Lotsa Washington County volunteers. Wouldn't worry my head none if'n I wuz you. They'll be in good hands."

"Good hands!" I thought Mama would burst. "They've gone off to war, Mrs. Jones! To fight!"

"Well, somebody gotta do the fightin'. Show them rich Southerners they can't live like lords ownin' negroes while the rest of us break our backs to make an honest livin'. We do all our work around here ourselves! What gives 'em the right to make others do fer 'em?"

"No right," Mama said. "But I am not here to discuss the politics of war with you."

"Ain't nuthin' t'do with politics," Mrs. Jones said flatly. "Got to do with right and wrong. My boys know wrong when they see it, and I'm right proud of 'em."

Mama was near distraught by now. "If you don't care about your boys, Mrs. Jones, I care about mine! Wes is too young! And your sons had no right influencing him to leave home against our wishes."

The woman turned away, walked back out onto the rock, picked up a shirt she'd been scrubbing, and wrung it out. "Lookee here, Mrs. Grafton. You've no call to take on like that. Weren't my boys who made up yer boy's mind fer him. He goes to that fancy St. James College, don't he? Well, then, he's got more brains than my two put together. Seems to me he should know his own mind."

"He's only sixteen," Mama said.

"I wuz fourteen when I wed my Harry." The shirt was shaken out now and laid on larger rocks in the sun with some others. They looked sootier, washed, than our laundry did before Mrs. Carmody scrubbed it. "I was 'bout the age of your young 'un here, yessir. And I've had nary a regret."

"Where is Harry?" Mama asked weakly.

"He took to the mountains yesterday. Huntin'.

Possum, deer, rabbits. We make our own way here, Mrs. Grafton. We live off the land. The land is good to us. We aim to keep it and not give it over to them Southern slavers. Now I'm understandin' yer grief over yer boy leavin'. But he ain't done nuthin' that any boy who's decent-raised shouldn't do. And as far as who gave who the idea to run off, my boys or your'n, well, far as I know my boys didn't have to hog-tie your'n. He wuz of his own mind. But that don't matter none. They's gone. Now if ye aim to carry on about it, ye kin leave. 'Cause I feel fer my boys just like ye do fer your'n. But if'n you aim to act peaceable-like, why I just might ask y'all to the house for some good apple cider and corn bread I got in the oven."

Her long speech finished, Mrs. Jones just stood there, her reddened hands resting on her apron front, staring at Mama. There was no sound for a moment, except the trickling of the water over the stones in the creek behind her.

"I have no time for cider," Mama said.

"Sure ye do. Ye got all the time in the world, if'n ye take it. I'm knittin' my boys some hose for the winter. They'll be writin' soon and lettin' me know where they's at. Soon's I hear, I'll tell ye. We may be mountain people, Mrs. Grafton, and you all fine town folk. But the way I sees it, those things don't matter none these days. Our boys knew enough to get shut of all that nonsense and go off fightin' together. So we may as well try to act as good as them, don't you reckon?"

Never, in all my life, had I seen Mama so taken aback, so speechless. I saw her run her tongue along her lips. I saw her heave a great sigh and wipe a tear from her eye.

"I'd be proud to have cider with you," she said softly.

So then the three of us went back to the house to sit on the porch and drink some cool apple cider, to eat some corn bread, and to speculate on when the boys would write to us. And would they have their tintypes done and sent home so we could see them in proper uniforms? There was no talk of war or where the battle that was surely coming hereabouts would be.

We left promising to keep in touch, to let each other know as soon as one of us heard from the boys. Mama did not say a word on the ride home. Just kept her hands, in her lace mitts, folded on her lap, her eyes straight ahead on the road, like she was in a velvet-tufted chair in some elite Hagerstown parlor.

I had some idea of what she was thinking. Or trying not to think. Mama was, after a fashion, a snob. All her life, she and Daddy had lived a certain way, abided by certain rules, associated only with certain people. And made sure Wes and I and Sky did, too.

In one fell swoop, beside a trickling stream, Mrs. Jones had disabused her of all her notions.

"Our boys knew enough to get shut of all that nonsense and go off fightin' together," Mrs. Jones had said.

It was hard to hear your way called nonsense. Hard to know the distinctions were blurred now, with the coming of the war. Hard to know all your notions maybe didn't hold anymore. I knew the feeling. Mama was confused. Well, so was I.

"Wes will be all right, Mama," I assured her. "He's right smart."

She smiled. But there were tears in her eyes. And I wondered what other notions we would have to throw out the window like some old bathwater before the war left us.

CHAPTER EIGHT

How Jinny Became Thriza and I Started to Wonder About Things

SEPTEMBER 14, 1862

The next day Mama insisted we go to church. We're Lutheran, and Reverend Austin has services both Sunday morning and Sunday evening.

After I put on my best calico and was on the way downstairs, I stopped and looked in Wes's room. There was nothing different about it. Yet his things seemed to stand out, like the things in the picture Mama had downstairs in the parlor. It was a copy of some famous work, and the title said something about the life in the picture being still.

Still what, I wondered. Still good? Still bad? I never understood what it meant. Now I did. Still life meant everything had stopped for the man whose clothing lay about his room in the picture. Did that mean that Wes's life was now still?

Church seemed awful crowded. Reverend Austin

should be pleased. But he didn't look it. He seemed cast down. Then I heard Mrs. Smith whisper as I passed, "Do you think he'll read the prayer for the president?"

Why wouldn't he? Reverend Austin always prayed for the president.

"He wouldn't dare," from Mrs. Hager. Both Mrs. Smith and Mrs. Hager were Southern sympathizers, and their sons had gone with the South.

I could name five such families before I reached our pew. Besides the Hager and Smith boys, Jim MacGill had gone with the South. Joe King and Reneh Small had gone for the Union. A lot of people in our congregation weren't talking to each other anymore.

Reverend Austin didn't know what to do about it. He was a strong Union man, but he never brought politics into church. Some parishoners were calling him mealymouthed. But I understood. He just didn't think it was his war yet, that was all. Why should a man of the cloth have to make it his war if he didn't want to?

Daddy said he shouldn't have to, that people went to church to be healed, not to get all fired up to kill each other. Daddy said God and love were Reverend Austin's stock-in-trade, and the smart man knew what his customers wanted.

Mama said church wasn't a store. "Anyway, look at Jesus," Mama would say. "He spoke out in the temple. He threw things and got angry." Mama held with getting angry at least once a year. She said it cleared the air.

The discussion was ongoing at our house and made for lively discourse. And it usually ended with Daddy saying we should have been Episcopal. Because their Bishop Whittingham had sent around circulars, forbidding omission of the prayer for President Lincoln at services.

While all these thoughts were crowding my head, Sky was nudging me and telling me to look, look.

"Look at what?" I whispered savagely. Then I looked. Rebel soldiers. At least two dozen of them, scattered in the congregation.

How dare they? I thought. How dare they take over our town and then come into our church?

"Mama," I whispered.

"Hush." She was reading her testament. I hushed and stole glances around me. Did soldiers go to church? Were these all Lutheran? They had their own testaments, too! Were they the same as ours? Was their God our God? If so, He was going to be even more cast down this morning than Reverend Austin. Whose prayers would He listen to?

I knew what I would do if I were God. I'd tell them

all to go away. Leave me alone. You started this war, now finish it on your own and don't ask me to settle your squabbles for you. That's what Mama said when I fussed with Wes or Sky. I couldn't concentrate with all those soldiers around us. Then it was time to sing.

"Rock of Ages." I loved that song. And apparently so did everybody else that morning, including the Rebel soldiers. They all joined in. Reverend Austin sometimes complained that our singing wasn't hearty enough. "If the whales that move in the water and the fowls of the air and the beasts and cattle can bless the Lord, why can't my congregation?" he scolded.

Well, that morning the Southern sympathizers, together with the Rebel soldiers, sang like the beasts and cattle. And the Union people started sounding like the whales and fowls of the air.

When the song was over, we heard the distant booming of the cannon from the direction of South Mountain. Everyone stood stock-still. It was time for Reverend Austin's usual prayer for the president of the United States. Would he say it?

I wished Wes were here. I'd make a whispered wager to him. Three jawbreakers saying Reverend Austin wouldn't say the prayer, for three jawbreakers from Wes saying he would. I'd end up with six jaw-breakers, I just knew it.

In the next instant, I lost all my jaw-breakers.

Reverend Austin said the prayer for Lincoln. Loud and clear.

I saw Mama smile. And right off, there was a mild disturbance. A rustling of dresses, coughs, clearing of throats, and the clanking of swords as some of the Rebel officers moved in their places. But at least everybody had the courtesy to let him finish.

When he did, there came a loud commanding voice from the back of the church. A man's voice. "Say a prayer for the president of the Confederate states!"

Nobody looked around. Reverend Austin just stood there, eyeing his people. And for a minute I thought he was going to start throwing things around, like Jesus. But he didn't have to. His gaze just held everybody. I don't know how long the moment would have lasted if the church door hadn't opened then. A Rebel sergeant came in. For a moment he just stood there, all backlit by the sun, like some avenging angel. Then he walked quietly up the aisle and whispered to an officer, who signaled with his hand, and, as if there had been a bugle call, all the Rebel soldiers up and left.

We stood like stone statues and watched them go. The booming of cannon from the distance got louder. The church doors were flung wide open, and we could see into the street, hear the sharp orders on the morning air, the bugles, the sound of men forming up, horses neighing, wagon wheels, horses' hooves, then the tramp, tramping as they marched off.

"It's started, God help us," a man said.

We filed out silently. When we got home, we found Jinny Pearl there. She never came of a Sunday, but Mama didn't seem surprised. "We've got lots to do, Jinny," she said.

"Yes, ma'am, I know."

How had Jinny known? Because she and Mama were of one mind now. Women. Knowing what they had to do. And right now it was cooking. I hadn't known. So I supposed I wasn't a woman yet. I felt outside their circle, even though I helped them cook all day, while the cannon fire filled our ears, all from the east of town. Sometimes it seemed as if the very windows rattled with the sound of it. Sometimes it was as if the ground itself were shaking.

Mama killed six chickens herself, and she and Jinny Pearl set to cleaning them. I was made to peel potatoes. A great ham was put in the oven.

"Why are we doing this?" I finally asked Mama.

"If you knock on any door in town right now, you'll find every other family doing it, too."

I thought that if there was all this cooking going on in town, it was because the women were hoping somebody would be alive to eat it. Then I thought about Josh. Later in the day, when the food was simmering on the stove, I asked Mama if I could go see him. She said yes.

"Take him a bit of ham and bread," she said. "But be back in time for evening services."

Evening services? I didn't think Reverend Austin would be able to stand any more. Didn't the people in this town ever get enough? I wrapped some food in a basket. Out at the front gate I found Sky, with an old pocket watch of Daddy's in his hand. "Want to come with me?" I asked.

"No. I'm counting."

"What?" The street was deserted.

"The artillery firing. It's coming at over a hundred shots a minute. Steady."

I looked down at my young brother, at his freckles, the blue eyes. There was a sharpness about his face that I'd never noticed before, as he peered at the hands ticking away on the old pocket watch. The war was ruining Sky. I wondered how soon it would be before he made it his war, too. I wondered why Mama didn't see it.

"How old do you have to be to be a drummer boy?" I asked Josh.

He shrugged. "If you can hold a drum, they take you."

"Don't the parents have to give permission?"

"Sure. But some young 'uns run off. I heard about an eleven-year-old who joined the 22nd Michigan."

"Sky is getting a real fix on the army, Josh. He sees a soldier, he doesn't care what side he's on. I'm afraid he'll run off. All he does is brag that his brother is a soldier."

We were sitting on some old chairs near the press. It was not only all put back together again, but Josh had polished up the medallions of Benjamin Franklin and George Washington in the circles on each side of the heavy cast-iron frame.

"Sky won't run," he said. "It's all just captured his fancy. He's living it out in his head. All boys live things out in their heads at that age." He sounded like a professor at Wes's college. "If the war wasn't going on, he'd make one up. This just makes it all easier for him, is all."

I nodded, feeling better. Josh always seemed to have a good answer for things, the reason being, I thought, that he was almost a man, yet still enough of a boy not to be covered with a man's tarnish. There were too many people around me who'd decided to become men before their time.

"So what have you been doing?" I asked.

He took another bite of the ham and bread. "Reading some. Any newspaper I can get my hands on. The judge and his wife have me over to supper two nights a week. I've been working on the press. I was counting on getting some wallpaper soon." He eyed me slyly.

"I forgot to look." I honestly had.

"The judge heard about a special train coming from Harrisburg, and asked friends there to send some newsprint. But the train got stopped at Angel's Cut north of town this morning by Confederates."

All the while we'd been talking, the sound of heavy firing in the distance had been constant. We'd tried to ignore it. But now it was getting very loud.

"When it's loud like that, it means General McClellan's army is being driven this way," Josh said. "And when it gets farther away, like now, did you hear that?"

"Yes."

"That means Lee's army is retreating."

"How do you know?"

He grinned. "It's the job of a newspaper man to gather information. I've been talking to Rebel guards. They said the Federals followed Lee and took Crampton's Gap. You know that commands the road to Hagerstown. I think they're pushing him back."

"I hope so," I said. "I know you're for the Confederates, Josh, but I hope so!"

"I'm not for anybody, Amelia. I know it's strange,

being that my father was for the South. But all I want right now is to print my paper and report things."

I stayed a while longer while he ate, but the cannon fire ruined everything. We both hunched in silence. Finally, he wiped his mouth and grinned. "You'd best get home," he said.

"I hope the train gets here with your newsprint. And I will try to find some wallpaper," I told him when I left. But I know he didn't believe me.

At sunset, when we went to church again, the bell was tolling mournfully. And the ground was still shaking. People gathered around out front, speculating.

They said our Union men had surrendered at Harper's Ferry to General Jackson. They said Lee was retreating, that all the Rebel pickets were gone from town. Indeed, there were none in sight. No sooner had the service started than we heard a commotion behind us. There, at the door, were at least two dozen soldiers. This time they were dressed in blue. Ours.

Reverend Austin invited them in. One handed him a piece of paper. We said our prayers and sang our hymns. Then Reverend Austin made an announcement.

"We've had word, dear people, that Confederate troops are streaming toward Sharpsburg. Two thousand passed by St. James College this day, and Mrs.

Kerfoot, wife of the rector there, stood the whole day handing out food and water. We have also had word that government supplies have failed to reach both armies. The men have had little more than hardtack for three days. They are in need of food."

He didn't say which men. And of a sudden, it didn't seem to matter. Everyone rushed out of church and home to bring out the food they'd cooked and load it onto wagons to take to the soldiers.

For the next two days, Lee kept at it. Guns continually boomed. House windows shook, rumors flew, and people cooked food and loaded it on wagons to take out of town, near the lines.

On Wednesday, the seventeenth, people started pouring out of town. Walking, riding horses, driving wagons. Sky ran outside to find out what was going on. He came back in to tell us that they were going to the top of South Mountain. "To see where Sunday's battle took place. Can I go, Mama? Can I?"

Mama said no. We'd cook, she said. Let others take the food to the battle scene. Meanwhile, Jinny Pearl was grabbing her shawl.

"I'm going, Mrs. Grafton." Her face was white and set. "I have to."

"All right, Jinny," Mama agreed. "But you may as well take some food in the wagon."

We loaded hams, chicken, beef sandwiches, crocks

of potatoes, bread, and jugs of cider into the wagon. Sky was beside himself at not being allowed to accompany Jinny, but Mama was firm. "I need you here to keep telling us what's going on," she said.

Mama and I went back into the house and she started ripping up sheets into bandages. Mama sat and rolled for half an hour in silence, while I cleaned up the kitchen. With every cannon shot, Mama jumped. Her face was so white, I was worried for her. Finally, I couldn't stand it anymore.

"I know you're worried, Mama. We haven't heard from Wes yet. He could have been in Sunday's battle. Why don't you go with Jinny? I can hold things down here."

"Jinny will find him if he's there" was all she would say.

She went on rolling. Then we heard Sky upstairs, yelling, "Fire! Fire!"

"That boy will be the death of me!" Mama threw down her roll of bandages, and we both ran upstairs.

Sky had climbed through the trapdoor in the attic that led to the roof. There he was, standing with a spyglass he'd taken from Daddy's desk. "There's a cloud of smoke!" He pointed in the direction of Sharpsburg. "Somebody's barn is on fire."

"Come in," Mama ordered. "Before you fall and break your neck."

We got Sky in, then went back downstairs. The wind changed, and we began to hear the roar of battle, a terrible sound. Even Sky was chastened by it.

Cannon, terrible in their booming, echoed off all the house windows in town. Even musket fire, and sometimes what we thought were the screams of either horses or men. It went on all day and into dusk, when we were eating a cold supper in the kitchen and heard a wagon pull into the side yard. We ran to the door.

Jinny Pearl was back with an empty wagon. Her apron and dress were splattered with blood. "He's not there, Mrs. Grafton. No sign of the Potomac Home Brigade."

"Thank the Lord," Mama breathed gratefully. "Come in, child, come in and clean up and have something to eat. You look exhausted."

Jinny washed up and sat down. Mama had to leave, to take the bandages she'd rolled to a neighbor woman, who would bring them to the nearest hospital that was being set up. She took Sky with her. I got Jinny a plate and sat at the table with her.

"Tell me," I said.

She shrugged and gave me a weak smile. "I was Thriza today."

"Thriza?"

"Yes. I came on a small log cabin, loaded with wounded Rebels. There were people all over South

Mountain. We'd heard thirty thousand were dead, but it looked like only about two hundred. There were about forty Rebels in this cabin, moaning and crying. People were doing the best they could, feeding them, giving them water. And all the while, you could hear the sounds of another battle going on over to Sharpsburg or Bakersville, or wherever it is."

I nodded.

"One of the young Rebels was dying. He looked right at me. 'Thriza,' he says, 'is that you?' There was a surgeon there, and I knew he couldn't do anything for the soldier. The surgeon just nodded at me to say yes. So I said yes. I knelt down beside him. I held his hand. 'Oh, I knew you'd come,' he told me, 'I knew you'd be here.'"

"Then what happened?"

"He died. But I comforted him first. I was Thriza."

"But he was a Rebel," I said.

"No matter." She wiped up some gravy in her plate with a piece of bread. "I'd want some Rebel woman to do it for Wes if he were dying. Wouldn't you?"

The horror of her words washed over me. But I could give her no reply. I don't think she expected any.

The next day word came to us that we had a great victory. And before nightfall, ambulances were coming to town with wounded and dying in them.

Mama decided, out of a clear blue sky, that she was going to work at one of the new hospitals. They were filling up with wounded.

"Do you think you should?" I asked. I knew Daddy wouldn't like it.

"It's the least I can do," she said. "Yesterday, I couldn't bring myself to go to the battlefield. I was afraid to go, afraid Wes would be there and I'd find him shot. Jinny wasn't afraid. What if Wes had been there, shot? Can I do any less than Jinny?"

"Jinny's different, Mama," I said.

She left me in charge of the house, and she and Jinny both went.

The Southern sympathizers were calling it the battle of Sharpsburg. The Union people, Antietam. Josh had told me that the North and the South had different names for all the battles so far, starting with the first. The South had called it Manassas, the North Bull Run.

Far as I was concerned, it didn't matter what they called this battle, but I thought both sides could at least agree on a name to an event in which they had killed each other.

Our town was in chaos. People were going to the battlefield in droves, trying to help, taking wounded soldiers into their houses, their barns, killing their livestock to provide more food. We found out that some were going to look for loved ones, and some were just wandering the wretched scene to pick the bodies clean of anything of value.

All the children in town were set to making bandages. They called it "picking lint." Mama left me in charge of Sky, too. I left him "picking lint" in the parlor and ran down the street to the newspaper office to see Josh for a minute. I needed to see him. He'd know just how great a victory it was. But he didn't answer my signal at the door. So I figured he must be out getting his story, which he would not be able to print, and I went back home.

I did my best, fixing supper for Jinny and Mama, and trying not to pay mind to the awful sounds coming from the ambulances in the streets as they went through with a new load of wounded. Sky kept running to the windows and coming back with reports. "Must be thousands dead!" he'd say with grim satisfaction. I made him come back and sit down and keep working.

Then, when it came time for the cow to be milked and the horses fed, I lost Sky.

One minute he'd been there picking lint in the parlor, the next, he wasn't. Well, I couldn't leave, could I? The supper would ruin. But I knew one thing. If he didn't get home before Mama and Jinny, I'd kill him.

Just about when it came on to dusk, he came

through the back door. In his arms he had his loot. A canteen. A Rebel cap. A bayonet.

"Where were you?" I demanded.

His face was smudged with dirt. "I went to the battlefield," he said.

"Well, the animals need tending. And I can't do that and make supper, too."

"I saw dead people, Amelia." His eyes were round and dark and glistening. "They were bleeding and ripped apart. There must've been thousands of 'em! You couldn't tell who was who. Which side, I mean. The doctors had tables set up right there and they were cutting off arms and legs. Men were screaming. I saw a pile of cut-off hands. I tripped over somebody's leg on the ground." His eyes were wide with the horror of it. But with the excitement of it, too.

"Oh, Sky!" I knelt down in front of him. But I could tell he wasn't seeing me. He was still seeing the arms and legs, the bleeding and ripped-apart men. He smelled, too. Of smoke, gunpowder, and something else. What?

Death, I decided. He smelled of death.

"You go wash up and change your clothes. We can't have Mama seeing you like this."

"Do you think Wes is ripped apart like that somewhere, Amelia?"

"No, I think Wes is fine and safe, and will soon come home to us."

"I saw dead horses, too. I felt bad for them. It wasn't fair. The men knew why they were there, but the horses didn't. Weren't right the horses had to die."

"No, it isn't," I agreed. "Now hurry. Mama will be home soon."

He nodded, then handed over his loot to me. "Do you think Mama will let me keep it?"

"No. I think you better hide it someplace so she doesn't see it. At least for now."

He agreed to that, too. In a little while, he was back down, face washed, hair slicked back, clean shirt and trousers on. He went out back to tend the animals, and then Mama came in.

"Jinny's gone home," she said. She looked terrible. She was pale, glassy-eyed. And her apron had bloodstains on it. She took it off and went upstairs to change. When she came back down, she could scarce eat. She just pushed her food around on her plate and stared a lot across the room at nothing. It was a quiet supper.

"Mama, I don't think it's such a good idea that you work with the wounded," I said.

"Why, I have to, Amelia." As if it was some truth I should have known all along.

"Why, Mama? Why do you have to?"

"I promised God."

Sky stopped eating and looked at her. So did I. "You promised Him what?" I asked gently.

"That I'd care for the wounded if He let Wes come through the war unharmed, honey. That I'd do my part, the way we all have to. And stop hiding away here making bandages."

What's wrong with hiding away here and making bandages, I wanted to say. They need bandages, don't they? But I didn't say it. "Why don't you go upstairs and rest, Mama," I suggested. "I'll make you a nice pot of real tea. And I've got some applesauce cake I made this morning."

"I don't know as we should use the real tea," she said. "We should save it for when someone gets ill and really needs it. Shouldn't we?"

You really need it, Mama, I wanted to say, but I didn't. I guided her out of the room, into the hall and up the stairs. I made Sky feed Duke and Duchess, let them run around the yard in back for a while, then bring them in for the night. I checked that all the doors were secure, and we went around and closed off the shutters. Then I got a tray of tea and cake for Mama.

If we'd had her silver tea set, I would have used it, because I think she really needed that, too. But I just knew we'd never see that tea set again. We hadn't seen

Aunt Charlotte since the day she took it, had we? Mama said she was busy supplying the troops with fruits and vegetables. No matter about the tea set. I just hoped we'd see Wes again.

I brought the tray upstairs, and when I went back down found Sky sleeping on the floor in the parlor with Duke and Duchess next to him. It was coming on to dark. I put a pillow under his head, covered him with a shawl, and took off his boots. Then I lighted one oil lamp and sat down with my own cup of tea. Except for the clock ticking in the hall, and the constant rumble of wagon wheels outside, it was quiet. It had started to rain — a soft, healing rain. I tried to read a book, but couldn't. I sat listening to the rain, and the rumble of wagons which had become part of it, part of the night, part of our town.

I set my book aside. I wondered where Aunt Lou was and thought how nice one of her biscuits would be right now with my tea. I thought about how happy Jinny Pearl had been being Thriza. She wants to do things, that girl, I thought. I wondered what she and Wes had fought over. Then I thought about Grandmother Schuyler, so far away in Philadelphia.

Funny, I hadn't thought about her in a long time.

I wondered when Daddy was coming home and why he hadn't written. If Mama would go to the hospital again tomorrow and how she could stand it if she did. I wondered why, all of a sudden, everyone had something to do in this war, and all I could do was cook. I wondered why that suddenly bothered me.

I thought as how I really should hunt up some old wallpaper for Josh. Then I got drowsy, but made myself stay awake at least until the clock struck nine. I waited. I don't know for what. But it seemed that someone should. It seemed the only thing to do.

CHAPTER NINE

The Woman on Horseback

MARCH 29, 1863

Amelia, go to the store this minute and tell your father that if he doesn't come home immediately, we will just go by ourselves to the celebration."

"All right, Mama."

"And go in the back way. I can't have any of our neighbors know your father has gone to do business of a Sunday."

"He isn't doing business, Mama. He's just gone to make sure everything is all right. You know people have been saying the Rebels are coming back again."

"The Rebels are not coming back, Amelia. Why would they, when our army drove them out last time."

"Mama, two weeks ago they were here."

"A band of marauders is all they were."

"Well, they stole a dozen of Adam Hutzell's horses."

"They aren't going to come here into town, not with the Union cavalry here. Now go, Amelia. And don't talk to any soldiers, Union or not."

I went. I was defending Daddy again. Well, it was something I'd become accustomed to. I'd defended him all winter from the snide remarks of the well-bred girls I went to school with, hadn't I? I went to school at the home of Mrs. Hiram Winchester now. Her husband was president of the seminary, and since war had closed it down, she'd offered to take in the first-year girls. There were ten of us. Of course, those girls had only said about Daddy what they'd heard their parents say.

That my daddy was making money on the war.

I never heard anything so stupid. Just because his store was doing well. Because Daddy knew what his customers wanted.

They wanted coffee, thread, needles, yards and yards of poplin, muslin, and calico. They wanted canned delicacies, candy, salt, combs, bonnets, shoes, shirts, hats, fresh produce, even ginseng, which his teamster picked up from mountain folk on the way down from Philadelphia where the rest of the goods came from.

Since he'd come home the previous November, with that first wagon load of merchandise from up North, many other wagon loads had followed, thanks to Grandmother Schuyler, who had "connections." Without her connections he could not have managed to get the merchandise through. Nobody asked how he did it. But other merchants in town couldn't get things, not even when the war left us last fall and winter. Gone to the west and the south. People were just jealous. But I noticed they weren't above buying what Daddy had. And glad to pay wartime prices, too.

Daddy tried to keep the prices down. But Mrs. Kealhofer came right out at a church social and insulted Mama about it.

"Isn't a shame some people are making a profit from the sufferings of others?" she said.

At first Mama cried. Then she threw Wes in Mrs. Kealhofer's face. She had a son off fighting. Did Mrs. Kealhofer? Then she'd waved some letters around. One was from Wes, who'd been detached from the Potomac Home Brigade and had been sent to Maryland Heights to fill out a brigade in the 7th Maryland.

The letter said, "Dear Mama, I wish you would send me something good to eat, for we don't get anything here but coffee and dry bread for supper, and bread and coffee for breakfast, and the leavings from dinner mixed with bacon fat. Please send butter and bacon."

It didn't work. "Well, you're lucky. You have them to send," Mrs. Kealhofer said.

We hadn't seen Wes since he'd left. Smallpox was rampant in the army, and he wasn't allowed to come home. No soldier was. The city council voted to send letters to their commanding officers, forbidding leaves. Then they voted that we all had to be vaccinated. Ugh! When I think about it! Sky and I had been sick for days!

Anyway, since the letter from Wes hadn't worked with Mrs. Kealhofer, Mama then produced the other letter. It was from forty Union soldiers in the Seminary Hospital, thanking Mama for her acts of kindness. Mama had worked harder than ever all winter in the hospital.

Jinny Pearl took it awful bad that Wes couldn't come home. At least, that's what I thought was plaguing her. She still came every day to help, but over the winter she'd become quieter and quieter, like she was going right inside herself and never wanted to come out again. Was it worry over Wes? She got letters from him, I know she did. And she wrote back. But she never told us what was in those letters. She never spoke of him. She was a peculiar one, Jinny Pearl. I still had the feeling there was more to her peculiarity than her secret about the dead Rebel soldier.

When I went in the back door of the store, there was Daddy, coat off, sleeves of his good Sunday shirt rolled up, wearing his long white storekeeper's apron and standing on a ladder.

He was putting the finishing touches on a large Union flag he'd painted on the ceiling. Right in the middle of the store, between the dry goods counter and the barrels of corn that he kept stocked for the Union cavalry.

He looked down and smiled at me. "How do you like it, Amelia?"

"It's right pretty, Daddy. But why?"

He didn't answer right off, but made some finishing touches on the stars, climbed down from the ladder, and stood admiring his handiwork. "Why? So all those busybodies who are giving your mother grief about my war profiteering can see it. That's why. Do you think your mother will like it?"

I wanted to cry. He'd come here on a Sunday, earning himself Mama's wrath, so he could give his detractors something to see. "Yes," I said.

"There's a certain poetic justice in the fact that when they come in here and buy my goods, they can do it while standing under our country's flag. Do you think they'll take notice of it?"

Take notice? I thought they would probably salute

it. I nodded yes. "Are you making money on the war, Daddy?" I don't know what gave me the mettle to ask it.

He turned to look at me, then went back to gazing up at the flag. "Yes, I suppose I am, Amelia," he said slowly. "To a certain extent. But I didn't drive up the prices. If I didn't bring my merchandise in, people in this town would be doing without. I have an obligation to serve my customers. So you'll have to decide for yourself about that."

He put his hand on my shoulder. "At least I'm not like the T. B. Spigler Company, offering tours of Antietam battlefield and charging people to take them. People hereabouts can go to the battlefield any time they wish. I'm not making excuses for myself, Amelia. But neither am I hurting anybody by taking advantage of my connections in the North, am I?"

"Mrs. Kealhofer never lets Mama hear the end of it."

"Well then, next time Mrs. Kealhofer comes in and asks for some poplin for a dress for Lutie, I guess I'll have to show her these barrels of corn I've been selling to the 12th Illinois Cavalry for less than I'd get on the peace market. Now, your mother sent you to fetch me, didn't she?"

"Yessir. She said you're to come right home."

He took off the apron and set it aside. "Important day today, Amelia," he said. "They're going to read the Emancipation Proclamation."

"Oh." Abraham Lincoln had signed it in January, freeing the slaves. It was all Mama and Daddy had talked about for a while. "Why now?" I asked.

"Well, Amelia, it seems there are some folks hereabouts who still don't believe the slaves are free. The city council discussed it and thought it a good idea."

He was on the city council. I wondered if it was his idea.

"Come on," he said, "we don't want to be late. I've got a surprise for everybody after the ceremonies."

"What?"

"Can't tell, or it wouldn't be a surprise, now, would it?" And he winked at me as we went out the back door.

The first thing Mama said when we arrived in our wagon at the large field at the south end of town was, "Such a crowd! I don't think this is a good idea, what with the threat of smallpox still around."

"People need to get out and mingle and have a good time," Daddy said.

The March day had turned balmy. Spring was in

the air, and people had assembled in a mood of festivity. Robert Moxley, who'd been a slave, had his negro band playing military airs on the field. With the Emancipation, they were now free. Would they stay in Hagerstown? Or leave? Would people now have to pay them for their performances?

Some people were hawking small American flags, others selling cold cider and sugar cakes. The field was crowded with soldiers in blue. The 12th Illinois Cavalry was up front, their horses all spiffed up and at attention. I thought Sky would jump out of his seat.

Robert Moxley's band played "The Girl I Left Behind Me," and "My Maryland." Then the men did drills. Then more music. Children sat on their fathers' shoulders and clapped and waved small flags. Most of the crowd was seated on blankets on the ground. Some, like us, were watching from their wagons.

Then, out of the corner of my eye, I saw the colonel of the 12th Illinois ride out onto the field on a handsome horse, flanked by two officers. But he wasn't alone.

At his side was a negro woman. She, too, rode a fine horse. She was dressed plain, but she wore a sparkling white apron and a red turban. She carried an American flag.

A ripple of murmuring went through the crowd as

the band played the national anthem and the negra woman rode slowly to take her place beside the colonel at the front of the troops. I heard gasps. "Who is she?" Mama gripped my arm and I felt a thrill of recognition.

Aunt Lou!

I muffled a squeal, then watched as Aunt Lou stood proud and erect, holding the fluttering flag while the strains of the national anthem floated on the air. The moment was filled with electricity. I felt raised above myself, in tune with the world and everyone around me. Then the colonel read the words of the Emancipation. When he finished I heard Daddy murmur, "Well, I knew she was coming, Leigh, but I never expected this."

"C'mon, Sky," I said. "Let's go welcome her proper-like. Can we, Mama?"

She had her handkerchief out. She was crying. "Go, yes, do. As soon as she finishes her duties."

We ran across the field, but had to push our way through a crowd to get to Aunt Lou. People were crowding around her, congratulating her. When we finally got through, she gathered us both in her arms. "I'se home for good," she said.

We lost Jinny Pearl after that. She didn't come to our house anymore, even though Mama said she still needed her. I thought she didn't want to play second fiddle to Aunt Lou in our kitchen. Then I thought she was jealous of the attention Aunt Lou had commanded that day on the field. But I was wrong on both counts. Oh, how wrong I was!

CHAPTER TEN

Good-bye to Jinny Pearl

JUNE 1863

I truly believe Belle Boyd was responsible for Jinny running away.

In the middle of June, our soldiers retreated north, when Confederate General Jenkins came into our town with two thousand men and sixteen pieces of artillery. Daddy left again. And Belle Boyd came to Hagerstown.

Word went round like a brushfire that she was here. Of course Lutie Kealhofer went and made a brass-bound fool of herself, presenting Belle Boyd with a key to the city and inviting her to their house for tea. I didn't go. Neither did Mama. Jinny Pearl did go, however. I found that out from Josh's "newspaper." He'd printed a small run on some old wallpaper I'd given him, wallpaper he'd saved up for a good story.

It was a good story, but I was a little put out with him. "You think Belle Boyd was worth the wallpaper?" I asked.

"Yes. Everyone wanted to know about her."

"I would think you'd want to save your newsprint for a battle."

"You're jealous of Belle Boyd," he accused.

"Why should I be?"

"Because she's doing something for the war and you're not."

Oh, that old argument. I flushed. "I think you were taken with her."

He grinned. "Hardly. But I know somebody you ought to be concerned about, who is."

"Who?"

"Jinny Pearl. She was there."

"Why should I care?"

Now he scowled. "When was the last time you saw her?"

"A month or so. She doesn't come around anymore."

"Then I think you ought to maybe ride out there and visit."

"Why? What's going on?"

"I don't know." He was solemn. "But something's going on with that girl. And since she's Wes's sweetheart, I think you should care."

"Don't you tell me what I should care about, and not care about, Josh. I don't need you to tell me that."

But I went.

Patches the dog came down the lane from the farmhouse, barking like I was a whole Confederate cavalry come to take their corn. Then, as I dismounted at the gate by the road, a shot rang out and zinged by my ear. It had come from the woods just to the side of the lane that led to the house.

I hid behind my horse. *There were Rebels here!* Then I heard Mrs. Beale yelling from the front porch.

"Jinny Pearl, we don't shoot at company!"

No more shots came, so I tied my horse to the gate post and walked up the lane. "Hello, Mrs. Beale."

She was shelling peas. "That girl's gonna get us in a heap of trouble one of these days. You all of a piece?"

"Yes, ma'am."

"Wish she'd just do what she's set her mind on and get it over with. She stays around here much longer, they're gonna hang us all."

The last time I'd seen Mrs. Beale was the day they'd been burying the soldier. Now she was neat and clean in calico and a fresh apron. She was a handsome woman, with just some gray in the shining dark hair. She rocked as she shelled, and I saw her as friendly. So I asked.

"What has Jinny got set in her mind to do?"

"You mean she didn't tell you?"

"No, ma'am."

"Ask her yourself, then, why don't you?"

I turned to see Jinny coming upon us. She was wearing boys' trousers, vest, shirt, and hat. One of her brothers' clothes. The musket was in the crook of her arm, and she was grinning. "Hey, Amelia," she said.

"Hey, Jinny."

"I was a ways back in the woods. Thought you were a Rebel. They've been stealing horses all over the place."

She looked like a man. Or at least a sixteen-year-old boy. Her hair was all tucked up under the hat, her stance, as she stood there grinning at us, was a boy's, not a girl's. I don't know what she'd done with her bosoms, because you couldn't see their outline under the shirt and vest.

"How do I look?"

"You look right fine, Jinny. I'd never have taken you for a girl."

"No girl round and about this whole county can shoot like I can," she said.

I stared at her, wondering what Wes would say if he could see her now. "Have you heard from Wes?" I asked.

"Two days ago. He wrote that they were abandoning their position on Maryland Heights and are preparing to follow new orders. He says the men are disgruntled. They liked General Hooker, but he's been replaced by Meade."

I was scarce listening. A spy, I thought. She's going to run off and be a spy.

"We miss you at home," I said lamely.

She stood there, the gun in one arm, patting Patches with the other. "I'm leaving soon, Amelia."

"Leaving?"

I saw the exchange of glances between her and her mother. Then Jinny walked up to the porch. "C'mon inside, and I'll tell you," she said.

"A soldier?" I gasped at her. "You're going for a soldier?"

We were upstairs in her plain, prim room that overlooked the barnyard. Out the window, I could see the white haze of the June heat across their cornfield, the blue-green mountain in the background.

She grinned at me. Then she pulled off the hat.

Her hair hadn't been tucked under it. Her hair had been cut short. It fell neatly, just under her earlobes, and was combed, on top, over to the side. She looked like a handsome boy.

"Jinny, your hair! Your beautiful hair!"

"It would only give me away."

"But why do you have to do this?"

"You've known all along I was going to do something. So did I. I just couldn't get a fix on what it was, is all. But I knew it wasn't sitting around here. Or helping Aunt Lou in your kitchen. Wes is gone. Putting his life on the line every day. So are my brothers. How can I live with myself and do less?"

"You're a woman, Jinny. Nobody expects it of you."

"I expect it of myself. The war has hurt us bad. My pa has to hide up the mountain. I can't pretend it doesn't exist, I have to do something. Sooner or later, we all have to." She stared at me with an unblinking gaze.

I flushed. "I suppose you're saying that on my account. Because I haven't made it my war."

"Just saying it. No cause to take on. It isn't your time yet, that's all."

"And what if I never think it's my time? What then?"

"It will be," she said softly. "When the time comes, you'll know it."

"Knowing it and doing right by it are two different things."

"You'll do right by it."

Her calm insistence was maddening. "You think you know so much!" I said.

She wasn't insulted. "Wish I did. Come on downstairs. I think it's time for me to show you something."

I felt foolish, being angry with her. "Jinny," I said. But then I couldn't go on.

"Yes?"

"What did you do with your bosoms? They don't show."

She grinned, flashing perfect white teeth. She was prettier now, I thought, with her short hair, than she was before. And she was pretty enough then.

"I bound them up. That's what all the women soldiers do."

"All?"

"There are others, Amelia. I'm not the only one. I've studied on it. A woman soldier was killed at Antietam last year. At the beginning of the war, a man with a Rhode Island regiment took his wife with him. She became one of the best sharpshooters. She fought at First Bull Run. So did Marie Tebe. She joined the 27th Pennsylvania and was in a lot of battles. There are others we haven't heard about yet, too. Word is just starting to filter out now."

"Does Wes know what you're about to do?"

"I always used to tease him about it. It's what we fought over, way back. It's why he went and did it first. Said he wasn't going to sit around and watch me make a dad-blamed fool of myself by running off as a soldier."

So, that was the trouble between them. "Your pa?"

"He knows, but only Ma understands."

"When do you go?" I asked.

"Tonight. After I bring Pa his supper." She scowled. "How did you get wind of it?"

"Josh. He saw you at the Belle Boyd celebration. Said you were so taken with her he feared you were about to do something foolish and that I should come visit."

"He's right smart, he is. Come on downstairs."

I followed her down the stairs, wondering what she was going to show me now. Another secret, she'd said. I half expected to find another dead Rebel in the kitchen.

But she led me into the parlor. On one wall was a massive stone fireplace and on either side of it were doors. She opened the one on the right-hand side, then leaned over and pulled up a trapdoor in the floor.

"This is the reason my pa is in hiding," she said. "And it's the reason he'll be arrested and jailed, and maybe even shot, if they catch him."

I peered down into the hole, trying to adjust my eyes to the darkness. "I don't see anything," I told her.

She sighed and closed the trapdoor, then turned to look at me. "Nothing there now. But there was before. Lots of times over these last few years."

"What?" I felt stupid.

"Runaway slaves. This house is a way station on the Underground Railroad."

I couldn't believe it! "My grandmother did that in Philadelphia!"

"They don't only do it in Philadelphia. They do it here, too."

"Other people?"

"Yes."

"Who?"

"I can't say. But you see now why I have to do something worthwhile? It runs in the family."

"What about your mother, left here after you go?"

"She won't leave Pa. Push comes to shove, she'll go to the mountain, too. It's all planned."

I stared at her, taking it all in. She was so far ahead of me. I felt myself lost in her dust. Jinny Pearl going for a soldier. I couldn't take it in. I left the Bealeses' under a blanket of gloom and hog-tied by promises Jinny made me swear to before she let me go.

She made me promise that I wouldn't tell anybody she was going for a soldier. Most of all, I wouldn't tell my folks. Especially Wes. She would tell Wes herself. In her own good time.

On the way back to town, I mulled the matter of Jinny in my mind. Why was I so angry about this? Because she was my brother Wes's sweetheart? Because Wes had joined up himself on account of it? No, because she made me feel guilty, was why. She was so brave. How could she be so brave?

And I was jealous. Her father was in hiding because he'd run a station on the Underground Railroad. My father because he was town treasurer.

There was nothing for it. I needed to talk to Josh.

I could see from the distance that there were no troops in town now. I looked right down North Potomac Street. It was hot, and dust was still rising from the street as if a horde of cattle had just come through. Then the dust cleared and I saw some horses hitched to the rail outside the market. And some men lolling around. It was too far to see whether they were Union or Rebel, but it was of no consequence to me at the moment.

Josh answered my two knocks immediately. "You shouldn't be out. The Reb army has been passing through all morning. They say sixty thousand will come through town in the next couple of days."

"Where are they going?"

"As far north as they can, I suppose, before the Union army stops them. You look cast down, Amelia, what's wrong?"

"I just came from the Beale farm. Jinny's run off."

"Where?"

"Her mother doesn't know. And her father's still in hiding. I think she must have run off to be a spy or something, Josh. It's all she ever talked about."

"That girl can shoot a musket better than most men hereabouts," he said. "Maybe she's run off to join the army."

I stared at him. He adjusted his specs, which were always slipping on his nose, and regarded me with a steady brown gaze. Did he know? He knew everything else that was going on in town. He was a walking town crier.

Then he smiled at me, and walked over to his father's large pigeonhole desk. He picked up a pile of paper. "These are my notes," he said.

"What notes?"

"I've been talking to everybody in town in my wanderings, and taking information. I've run out of paper, but at least I'll have my notes when all this is over."

"I don't have any more wallpaper to give you, Josh."

"I know."

"What's going on at the market house?" I gave the conversation a new turn.

"It's filled with rations for Lee's men. His army just about ate their way through Virginia, and I understand there wasn't much to eat there to begin with, and they're all starving. Heard tell that they've seen our wheat all ripe and cut and have been pounding on doors and making the women get up and bake them loaves of bread on the spot. Even if it's the middle of the night."

"I saw there's no Union flag flying in front of the courthouse."

He nodded. "You missed all the fun. Couple of hours ago the 4th North Carolina came through and cut down all the Union flags over the stores and houses. You know Mrs. Hammond, who lives in the old Hager House?"

"Yes."

"I stopped by there this morning. She's so scared of the Confederates, she's hiding in her chimney. Her husband had his horses and other critters in the cellar. A spring runs through it."

Josh had a pad and pencil. He never seemed to be without one, anymore. He was drawing General Lee as he spoke, and from what I could see, it was a good likeness. Well, he had talent as an artist. He'd sometimes drawn cartoons for his father's paper before the war.

"On Prospect Street, some people threw eggs down from their housetops at Rebel soldiers this morning. And there's going to be a big battle somewhere north of us, Amelia." Now he was sketching Lee's horse, Traveller.

I nodded and waited.

"From what I've seen of Lee's army, it looks good. Better than when they were here last year. They have real discipline."

"What are you trying to tell me, Josh?"

He stopped drawing. "Lee needs a victory on Northern soil. He needs it to have the Confederacy recognized in Europe. He needs help from Europe."

I nodded solemnly. "Do you want him to win?"

"It isn't what I want that matters."

"But do you?"

He thought for a moment. "Sure. I've got Southern leanings." He pulled something out of his pocket. "I had a letter from my father. He's in Detroit, with his brother. I've had letters before, of course, but I haven't answered them. I think I'll answer this one. I've come round to thinking that just because he signed the oath of allegiance to the Union doesn't mean he wasn't brave."

"Of course not."

"There are different kinds of bravery. We're all given different things to stand up to. So, anyway, I'm glad you came today. I needed to talk to you."

I had needed him to help me. I still did. And I felt empty and cheated as I left the store. I suppose having friends doesn't always mean they have to be there for you. Sometimes you have to be there for them. Just when you need them most.

I rode off. Passing by Daddy's store, my spirit flagged. It gave me the blue devils to see the shade pulled down on the front door, the "closed" sign in the window. I missed Daddy so bad, sometimes I wanted to die.

CHAPTER ELEVEN

Meeting General Lee

I got home to find more confusion. Aunt Lou was hitching up the wagon, and Mama was running from it back into the house and out again in enough of a dither to make me think the Rebels were in our back garden.

"What's wrong?" I asked Aunt Lou.

"That brother of yours. He done run off."

At first I thought they were speaking of Wes. Had he been hurt? "Has Mama had news of Wes?"

"Not him, the other," Aunt Lou said. "He done run off to join General Lee."

I stood rooted to the spot. "Sky's joining the Rebel army? As a drummer boy?"

Mama came out of the house. "He has not joined the Rebel army. He was invited to Lee's camp."

"Invited?" I thought she was touched by the sun. Or weakened by too much work at the hospital.

"We are all invited," Mama said. "Your father served in the old army with Lee in the Mexican War, remember. I'm sure it was just courtesy on Lee's part. I wrote a note, declining, but Sky went as soon as I turned my back. And now we must make our appearance. And fetch him."

"He took my bucket of raspberries," Aunt Lou muttered. "To give to Lee. It took me all mornin' to pick 'em."

I think Aunt Lou was more upset over those raspberries than anything. Mama, meanwhile, ran into the house two more times before we left. Once for her good straw hat to ward off the sun. And a second time for her silk shawl to keep from getting chilled.

If I hadn't known better, I'd have thought Mama was in a dither because she was going to meet the great general of the Southern cause. And not because Sky had run off and needed fetching. But I knew better. Of course I did.

By the time we got to General Lee's camp in the grove of hickory trees on the pike, I'd changed my mind again about Mama. She was wearing her blue silk. And her best shoes, the ones Daddy had ordered for her from New York City. They were pure kid. I think it was when she drew her lace mitts out of her reticule that I admitted to myself that she was all gussied up to meet Lee.

We passed through the sentries guarding the entrance to the camp, and Aunt Lou guided the wagon under a tree to the place we'd been assigned. I climbed out and helped Mama down. That's when I smelled the lavender water on her person.

"Fix your hair," Mama said to me. "You are about to meet an old army superior of your father's. We have our position to uphold. And if he speaks to you, call him sir."

"Do I have to curtsy?"

Mama hesitated for just a moment. "Yes," she said. "If he can extend an invitation to us, knowing we are on opposite sides, we can keep the social graces alive. That's one of our duties as women, Amelia. Keeping the social graces alive. Aunt Lou?"

Aunt Lou was hanging back, behind the wagon. I could tell this expedition was painful for her. How could it not be? This was the camp of the man who was the leader of the army fighting to keep slavery. But she must have had mixed feelings, too. Because when Mama said that about upholding our position and meeting Daddy's old superior, she took me in hand.

First she loosened the bow I wore at the end of the one long braid down my back. Out of Mama's reticule came a comb, and there under the trees, in full view of some nearby Confederate soldiers, who were standing around holding their horses' reins and jawing away the afternoon, I had to have my hair combed out loose around my shoulders. Then, from the bed of the wagon, where it had escaped my eye, Mama drew out a fresh white pinafore-apron. "Put it over your dress."

I stood stubbornly. "I won't get fussed up for Lee."

"You'll do it or sit right here and wait for us," Mama decreed. "But be informed. Lutie Kealhofer was out here in camp this morning. She met not only Lee, but Longstreet. Besides, I need you with me, Amelia. Don't abandon me now. Do you think this is easy for me?"

Ashamed, I allowed myself to be fussed up for Lee. I put on the pinafore and followed Mama past the group of cavalry officers and their horses, and to a grove of hickory trees where Lee's marquee was set up. It was a colorful scene, like something out of a book that told about knights of old.

There was Lee on a camp chair, surrounded by his dashing officers. There were orderlies holding the reins of horses that grazed on the emerald-green grass outside the pleasant circle. There was a table set with a white cloth and china. A number of men were seated around a long table. They didn't resemble any Confederate soldiers I'd seen so far in the war. Their trousers and jackets were of the softest gray fabric, their sashes bright, their boots shined to a fare-thee-well and sword hilts gleaming.

They looked like they were gathered for an afternoon tea at the seminary. Cups clinked in saucers. Talk was soft. So was laughter. It was very pleasant, until I realized that they were making plans for war. And what that meant to me at the moment was that they were making plans to kill my brother Wes.

What are we doing here? I asked myself. And then I saw Sky, standing next to Lee, who was listening to him intently. They all were. Sky was holding court.

I heard Mama gasp. "A vexation to me," she said again. Then she sallied forth to uphold our family position. At the same time, an officer saw us approaching and came to greet us. I held back with Aunt Lou while the officer bowed, then took Mama to Lee.

Immediately Sky stepped aside and Lee stood facing us, watching Mama's approach.

"This is Mrs. Grafton," the officer introduced Mama. "She's come to collect her son."

"Madam." Lee bowed.

I held my breath, wondering if Mama would

curtsy. She did not. She gave Lee her hand, allowed it to be kissed, and held herself straight. Good for you, Mama, I thought.

"I hope he hasn't been a nuisance," Mama said.

"To the contrary," Lee answered in a soft drawl. "He has kept us all most entertained, and served to remind us of young ones we left at home. We all miss our children. Your Schuyler has given us a pleasant hour of diversion from the grim business of war. I'm so glad you decided to come, Mrs. Grafton. Is your husband keeping? I remember him so well from the Mexican engagement."

Mama said something about Daddy being out of town. Lee called an orderly and ordered tea. Mama declined, but Lee insisted. Then he looked at Sky. "Would you like to get on that horse over there while I chat with your lovely mother?" he asked.

The horse in question was gray. And Sky's eyes nearly came out of his head. "Is that Traveller?"

"No other," Lee assured him.

The look on Sky's face as he was led off by an officer to climb on Traveller's back was the look one would wear at walking through the pearly gates of heaven.

A camp chair was pulled out for Mama, whose silk dress rustled most impressively as she sat down. "This is my daughter, Amelia, General Lee," she said holding a lace-mitted glove out to me. So I was made to step forward.

Mama gave me a look. So I curtsied. Then what was I to do? Oh, I wished I were older, wished I were Lutie Kealhofer. I bet she'd known what to do.

Better yet, I wished I were Jinny. She'd sung "The Star-Spangled Banner" in his face. Oh, I was good for nothing, is what I was! I didn't know how to flirt, and I didn't know how to stand up for what I believed in.

Lee nodded and smiled and acknowledged me with a nod. "Lovely," he said. "Your husband must be proud."

His eyes were piercing blue. His hair pure white. All done up in his uniform, with his sword, he looked like some avenging angel. Only a sad one, I think. There was much sadness in those eyes. He turned from me then and sought the eyes of another officer, who pulled out a chair and gestured I should sit. I did.

"You have a lovely family, Mrs. Grafton," Lee was telling Mama.

"Our son is off fighting," Mama told him. She did not say on which side. Did she assume he knew? Did he know?

"All our sons are fighting," Lee said. "My Rooney was just wounded at Brandy Station a few weeks ago.

At South Mountain, last year, he was unhorsed and knocked unconscious."

Tea and cake were served. Mama and General Lee spoke of family. She inquired after his wife, who was an invalid, sounding like a neighbor, someone who lived across the creek from him. He remarked on our countryside. "Most all my men are north for the first time and are greatly taken with your lovely homes, your neat barns, your fields of wheat and corn here in the Shenandoah Valley."

Mama thanked him. As if it were *her* valley.

I drank my tea, ate my iced cake, tried not to steal sidelong glances at the officers who surrounded Lee, all tall and handsome and dashing, staying a discreet distance away, yet alert for any sign from him. But the rest of the visit was a blur. My thoughts were muddled.

Out of the corner of my eye, I saw Sky on Traveller, saw him lifted down by an officer, allowed to hold the man's sword. I saw troops passing on the pike in the distance, under a cloud of dust. Lee's troops, come to invade us while he and Mama took tea. It was all like a dream. I wondered what Mrs. Kealhofer would say when she heard about this. And hear she would, the way news got around Hagerstown.

I wondered what I would tell Josh. I should be listening and paying mind, so I could tell Josh things. I should be listening, instead of acting like a silly girl. But I just couldn't sort out the patchwork quilt of colors and tableaus around me. It was all too much to take in.

Next thing I knew, it was time to go. Mama was getting out of her chair, Lee standing and doing more bowing. In the distance I saw Aunt Lou gathering in Sky, saw an officer hand her back the empty basket.

Aunt Lou had taken Sky's hand and was walking back to our wagon. A gig drawn by a fine-looking horse had just pulled into camp. As we walked to our wagon, Doctor Doyle, who'd been driving the gig, was coming toward us, and Lee going to meet him.

They shook hands. As I passed them, I heard Lee thank Doctor Doyle for coming. Then they started talking.

I lingered. I bent down as if to fix my shoe.

Lee was asking Doctor Doyle about the roads hereabouts. Were they in good order this year?

I unbuttoned and took off my left shoe, shaking it as if it held a pebble. Then I put it on again and began buttoning. I was a good-enough distance from them. But I could hear.

Lee had taken a map from his coat pocket. "What road runs to the Leitersburg pike?" I heard him ask.

"Does the Cavetown pike cross the mountain? What kind of crossing could one expect? Will my right flank be protected by the Blue Ridge until I reach Gettysburg?"

I couldn't prolong the business with my shoe forever. Besides, Mama was calling. I ran to the carriage.

Gettysburg! I couldn't wait to tell Josh! That was Pennsylvania! My daddy was in Pennsylvania. How far was Philadelphia from Gettysburg?

"What did you think of Lee, Mama?" I asked, as the wagon pulled out onto the pike.

She looked at me. "I wish he were ours," she said.

Nobody spoke much on the way home after that. We were all spent. Sky fell asleep in the wagon, no doubt dreaming of being on Traveller's back. He would be impossible to live with from here on, I decided. Impossible.

CHAPTER TWELVE

Gettysburg, and What Came After

THE FIRST WEEK IN JULY, 1863

A few days later we heard the guns booming in the northeast, like some giant was coughing in the mountains. Confederate cavalry came through town. Then the Union cavalry. All we heard was the tramping of feet, the lively fifes and drums. We went on with our lives. Mama spent whole days at the hospital, making good on her promise to God. I think she thought Wes was in the battle. Women were cooking again, and I was set to helping Aunt Lou.

There are moments from those days that will stay with me forever.

I remember the emptiness of the town, the merciless heat baking us. Aunt Lou made gallons of lemonade and stored it in the springhouse. I remember Mama giving me and Sky money and letting us go to the drugstore for a soda. Mr. Augenbaugh kept looking out his windows and wiping the counter. He had a glazed look in his eyes.

"Tell your mama all communication's been cut off," he said. "The people who tried to leave on the cars this morning for Baltimore had to come back. The rail lines are torn up in Frederick. And the telegraph lines are cut. We've got no communication with the North. We're part of the Confederacy now, and will be until the outcome of the battle is known."

Part of the Confederacy. I didn't like the ring of it. Mr. Augenbaugh all the time kept wiping the counter. Then he gave us two extra scoops of ice cream and wouldn't take our money.

Everybody was conjecturing about where the battle was. I supposed it was Gettysburg. That was where Lee was headed, wasn't it? I'd told no one, not even Josh, what I'd heard him say. And I felt guilty knowing. So I kept myself busy. Besides helping Aunt Lou, I made special delicacies for Mama.

I remember how welcome the dark was when it came on the first of July. It brought the first break from the heat. And silence of the cannon. All our neighbors came out into the street just to see each other, to speculate about what was happening. Was it over? Who had won? Why were there no couriers? Then we saw Mayor Ratliff coming down the street.

My hands got clammy. Yet I had chills. Somehow Mayor Ratliff had found out that I knew where the battle was all along. And he was coming to arrest me because I hadn't shared what I knew.

It turned out all he wanted was to tell us that the July Fourth celebration was cancelled. Nobody had expected it to be held.

The next day the cannon started again. More heat, more clouds of smoke over the mountains, more speculation, more hand-wringing and cooking. We prayed for nightfall, we prayed for cool breezes, we prayed for rain. We prayed that Wes wasn't there.

Sky spent the whole day on the roof, scanning the horizon. The worst part of it all was what we did not know. Were we still part of the Union? Or did we now belong to the Confederacy?

On the third day of the battle, I ran out of chores and so I set myself to making cookies. As the cannon boomed I rolled out my dough, wondering if Wes was there. Or Jinny. And where Daddy was. By dusk rumors were flying through town. We had lost, and Lee was on his way to Washington to take over the White House. We had won and Lee was dead.

Mama came in late from the hospital and went right to bed. I went into the closet in the hall, found

Daddy's winter duster, and buried my face against it, wishing he was home.

I remember the rain. And I remember Elizabeth Fiegley.

The rain started on the Fourth of July, after the cannon stopped, a soft, forgiving rain that went on all night. I awoke to it on the morning of the fifth. It pinged off the gutters and filled our rain barrels. In the kitchen, Aunt Lou had all the lamps lit, and it was downright cozy. I poured myself a cup of coffee, put plenty of milk and sugar in it, and sat down to watch her as she worked. Her beaten biscuits were in the oven.

"Aunt Lou," I said, "do you hear anything?"

"What am I supposed to be hearin'?"

"There are no cannon. It's past seven, and there are no cannon."

"I expects this rain has washed them all over the mountains."

"Aunt Lou, what will you do if the North loses?"

"Ain't thought about it, chile."

"They'll send you back to slavery."

She stood by the stove, one hand on her hip. "They can try," she said.

I thought that if the North lost, we'd have to hide Aunt Lou. I wished we had a trapdoor that led to a secret hiding place in the floor like Jinny had. No, we'd smuggle her to Philadelphia, to Grandmother Schuyler's. She'd hide her. But if the North lost, wouldn't Philadelphia be under Confederate rule, too? Oh, I was so confused!

"Now I hears somethin'," Aunt Lou said. "Who could that be?"

Someone was knocking on the front door. "I'll get it," I said. I started into the hall.

"You look out that curtain first and make sure who it is," she called after me.

I could scarce see, the rain was pouring down so. It was a woman. She had a shawl covering her head. I opened the door a crack. "Yes?"

"I'm Elizabeth Fiegley," she said.

I recognized the name, but I didn't know why. "What can we do for you?"

Mama was coming down the stairs. "In heaven's name, let her in."

I did so. The woman stepped just inside, fearful of dripping. "Thank you, Mrs. Grafton. I knew I could depend on you. No one else will answer the door to me this morning."

"How can I help you, Elizabeth? Are the children all right?"

"The children are fine, all home. It's just that I have a bit of intelligence. And like I said, no one will open the door to me."

"Yes?" Mama's face looked strange. I could tell she was thinking it was bad news.

"I had a gentleman caller in the early hours of the morning. He writes for *Harper's*. He was at Gettysburg. Where the battle was. He said it's over. And we won. The Union won, Mrs. Grafton. I wouldn't tell Mayor Ratliff. Wouldn't give that man the right time of day. Not after he issued an order to stop me from being around town hall and all."

I still didn't know who this woman was, but of a sudden Mama hugged her, wet as she was. Just hugged her, then me. "Aunt Lou!" she called out. "Get Elizabeth Fiegley a towel. And set out another plate for breakfast."

"Oh no," Mrs. Fiegley said, "no need."

Mama insisted. But Mrs. Fiegley declined again. "I have to get home to my children."

"Then we'll send something home with you. What do you need?" Mama asked.

"Nothing, Mrs. Grafton, for sure. All I need is for you to get the word out. Though I don't know why I care. The people in this town have their noses so high in the air, I'm surprised they haven't drowned in the rain."

"I could send my cookies for the children, Mama," I offered.

"Yes, do. Go get them all. Wrap them good," Mama ordered.

I ran back into the kitchen to fetch my cookies. "Who is this woman?" I asked Aunt Lou.

"Best let your mama tell you." And she went out into the hall with a mug of hot coffee. I followed with my cookies. Mama had fetched a dry shawl and an umbrella, which she insisted Elizabeth Fiegley take. She sipped some coffee, then Mama hugged her again as she went out the door.

And so it was that we found out the result of the battle, before anyone else in town, even Mayor Ratliff. From Elizabeth Fiegley, the town's fancy woman.

That's what Mama told me when I asked. She was the town's fancy woman. That's all she would say. It was why the mayor had evicted her from the town hall.

I didn't think she was dressed so fancy. Then I figured the mayor was just jealous. Because she was prettier than his wife, any day.

They called it the Battle of Gettysburg. Both sides called it that. No arguments this time. Not after what had happened there. The North and the South finally agreed on something.

Then, just when we thought it all over, it began again.

They came at eleven in the morning on the sixth.

Mama had sent me and Sky out to pick up the yard, which was full of twigs and small branches blown off the trees. It was a nice morning. I remember having a bundle of small twigs in my hands and going to a barrel near the front of the house.

Over the picket fence in front, I came face-to-face with a soldier. For a moment we just stared at each other. He looked spent. He had three or four days' worth of stubble on his face. His eyes were red-rimmed. His uniform was dirty, but I could see it was a butternut color. And he wore an insignia. It said "13th Virginia."

"Hello there, little lady." He tipped his hat. "You wouldn't have a bit of breakfast left over, would you?"

"Sky! Sky!" I dropped the bundle of twigs and ran to the back of the house.

Mama heard me and opened the side door. "What's wrong?" Then she saw the soldier, too.

"Howdy, ma'am."

Mama drew us close. "Are you lost?"

"No, ma'am. We're in town."

"We?" mama asked.

"Yes, ma'am. The 2nd North Carolina, the 10th and 13th Virginia. Chambliss is our commander. We've got our pickets all over the place."

"We heard the battle was over at Gettysburg. Why are you here?"

"Why, to take a stand, ma'am." He was so polite he even held his hat in his hand. "When the Yankees come after us, we aim to take a stand. Right here."

"But this is our town," Mama insisted. She could not accept that they were here.

"Yes, ma'am," he said gently, "but now I'd advise you all to go in the house. There's gonna be a fight."

"A fight?" mama asked. "Here? In front of our house?"

"A fight wherever we have to make it a fight," he replied. "I'm sorry, ma'am. It's nothing personal."

"You have brought the war to our town," Mama flung back tearfully. "And you say it's nothing personal? You people have been tramping through our town for over two years now. Why can't you leave us be?"

"I suggest you all get into the house and close up tight," he said patiently. ·

Then, in the next minute, we saw more soldiers in butternut, creeping around, holding muskets. And some on horseback. Mama pulled us into the house. "Close the shutters," she ordered, "quickly. Sky, run out and lock the barn door. And bring the dogs in the house."

In a little while we could hear shouts and gunshots. Mama wouldn't let us near the windows. She went and got a supply of sheeting. I don't know where

Mama got all this sheeting that she rolled into bandages. She had a whole stack of it.

She made Sky and me sit in the parlor and roll bandages. She and Aunt Lou set themselves to cooking. The kitchen was loud with sounds of chopping, of frying. In a little while Sky slipped away. I knew where he was going: upstairs with Daddy's spyglass, to the roof. I didn't tell on him, because I wanted to know what was going on, too.

It went on all morning. Thundering horses' hoofs, the rumble of wagons, shouts, curses. Then gunshots. Sometimes we'd hear a window smash.

Mama asked me once, "Where's Sky?"

"He heard a shutter banging upstairs and went to secure it." The lie came so easily.

In a little while, Sky came down. "There's fighting on Baltimore Street," he whispered to me. "And on the town square. They're fighting hand-to-hand on the square, Amelia. I could see them."

"Who's winning?" I asked.

"I can't tell. But suppose they win, Amelia? Suppose they take the town? What then?"

"We should prepare to leave," I said. "If only for Aunt Lou. First thing they'll do is send her back to slavery."

"Let's tell Mama," he said.

So we told her. "All right," she sighed. "Amelia, you

161

go upstairs and put together some blankets and clothes. But how will we know when to leave?"

"I can keep lookout," Sky offered. "From the roof. I know how to tell if things are turning against us, Mama."

"And how will we get away?" she asked.

"The wagon," I answered. "I can hitch it up, and we can take down the fence behind the barn. There's a path there that leads out of town. Through the woods. Nobody will see us. If they win, we have to go, Mama. We can take the livestock. I know the way Daddy goes to Philadelphia."

"I can lead the team and have us over the Pennsylvania line tonight," Sky said.

Mama hesitated.

"Daddy would want it," I persisted.

"My darling children." Mama held out her arms and embraced us. "I'm so proud of you both. Keep a lookout and tell me when you think we should leave."

The minute we were out of her sight, Mama's darling children had a fight. "I want to look through Daddy's spyglass, too," I told him.

"Ma said you should get the clothing together."

"I'll get mine and Mama's. You can get your own. Then I want to look through the spyglass." In no time at all, I had clothing tied up for myself and Mama. I think Sky threw together a shirt and some breeches. When I got to the roof, he was peering through the spyglass.

"A blue soldier just went down in the street, right in front of our house," he said.

"Give it to me."

"You're a girl. You wouldn't know a blue soldier from a Reb."

"I know more than you think, Schuyler Grafton." I reached for the spyglass. We fought for a moment, but I was stronger and wrenched it from him.

"Go ahead," he sneered. "You'll never figure out what you see."

I looked through the spyglass. "There's lots of blue soldiers around now. Our side isn't giving up so easily. Soldiers are on the pike to Funkstown and Boonsboro. There's a fierce fight at Baltimore and South Potomac Streets. Sharpshooters are firing out of people's homes." I recited without hesitation. "More of our soldiers are coming, in force, Rebels are hiding in alleyways and behind trees. The front windows of Marshall and Cranwell's Hardware Store are smashed. So are the windows of Andrew Hager's Feed Store."

"All right, all right," Sky said disgustedly. "Let me have a turn now."

I lowered the spyglass, but held it close to me. "Take back what you said about my being a girl."

"How can I? You are one."

"You know what I mean. Take it back!"

"All right. I take it back. Now can I have the stupid spyglass?"

I handed it over. "There's dead and dying all over," he said.

I could see some of it without the spyglass. I couldn't believe the view we had. I could see the rooftops of all the houses and stores, the church steeples, the streets laid out in careful patterns, puffs of smoke from the guns, clusters of soldiers forming up, kneeling to fire. I could see some creeping around in our churchyard, even hiding behind tombstones.

It looked not quite real. I couldn't believe this was our town. It looked so beautiful from up on the roof, like a picture from a book. I'd never known it was so beautiful, with the fields and farms around it like a patchwork quilt. A feeling of pride flooded me. And anger. I wanted those Rebel soldiers out of here.

"What kind of guns are those, on the seminary grounds?" I asked Sky.

"Parrott guns."

In the next instant, we saw the discharge as they went off, the spewing of smoke and fire, the rocks and dirt they unearthed. Then we heard the huge, roaring sound.

"Ours or theirs?" I asked.

"Ours, I think."

Then, on the street, about two blocks from the square, I saw blue soldiers. Some officer was riding right down the middle of the street, going to the square. I could see that Rebels held the square. The officer was in full view of them, riding right toward them. But he had men on either side, backing him up.

"Give me the glass," I said.

Sky handed it over.

"The Rebels are firing at him!" I told Sky. "No, wait, his men are firing back."

I saw Rebels jumping the stone wall of the Dutch Reformed Church yard, to hide behind it and fire. The blue soldiers were still going forward. They were near the market house now. The Rebs were firing on them. "Oh, the officer is hit!" I grabbed Sky's arm.

He took the glass. "His men have him out of the saddle," Sky said. "They're retreating, carrying him off."

I wondered where God was and why He hadn't protected that blue soldier. Couldn't God see He was trying to get the town square back from the Rebels?

What was wrong with Him, anyway? Whose side was He on?

It went on all afternoon, but soon Mama made us go downstairs. Enough war, she said, we'd have nightmares. She had a headache from the gunfire and the tension, so Aunt Lou made her lie down with a cool rag soaked in vinegar on her head. There was nothing else we could do. We waited. I wandered, fidgeted, patted the dogs who crowded close to me, whining nervously with every boom.

Mama dozed. Aunt Lou was in her room off the kitchen, packing. Sky stayed in his room. I sat on the stairs near the landing, the dogs next to me. They kept whining. Duke tried to hide his face in my dress. Duchess sat with her face to the wall, disgusted with the whole human race. I didn't blame her one bit.

After a while, I leaned against the wall, too, with Duke's head in my lap. I dozed, saw fleeting faces in front of my mind. I heard Jinny's voice, then, Wes's. I saw Daddy painting the flag on the ceiling of the store.

I was jolted awake by a thundering cheer outside. The house seemed even darker than before. I set Duke's head aside and yelled to Sky. "What is it?"

He came scrambling down the stairs and peered out the front window. "Jeb Stuart," he said.

"Jeb Stuart?"

"Lee's best cavalryman. He just came through, and all the Rebs cheered him.

"Are they winning?" I thought I couldn't take any more. I wanted to jump out of my skin.

"No."

"Then why are they cheering?"

"Rebs cheer," Sky said. "It's what they do."

I went into my bedroom and checked my bundle of clothes. After a while, I heard the downstairs clock chime five. The dogs would have to go out and relieve themselves in the yard. I started out of my room. I was at the top of the stairs when the front door opened. It was Sky.

"You were outside?" Mama was dismayed.

"It's over," Sky said.

"Who won?" Mama asked.

"The Confederates are in town," Sky said. "But I don't think they won."

"Then why are they still in town?" Mama asked. "If you lose you leave. Why don't they ever leave?"

"It doesn't work that way." Sky explained. "You don't just go when you retreat. You try to make some kind of a stand. But it isn't working. I heard on the street that Lee's army is trapped near Williamsport. He can't get over the Potomac because it's flooded.

And I heard that our cavalry is advancing on him."

"Good," Mama said. "Then we don't have to leave, do we?"

"I don't think so," Sky said. "I think Lee has his own problems. I heard he's hoping people will help the wounded. There are women in the street already, helping the soldiers."

This was just what Mama needed to spur her into action. "We'll be needed outside. Aunt Lou," she called. "Fetch the water and bandages." She and Aunt Lou went out the front door. All up and down our street, women were coming out to give aid to the wounded and dying.

It had clouded over and was starting to drizzle rain again. Light spilled out from the houses. Stray horses stood with downcast heads, and women moved about amongst the men, bending, administering, offering help. Somebody brought a wagon.

"The Washington House," I heard a man's voice cry. "And the Franklin House Hotel." It was Doctor Simmons. He was directing things, overseeing the loading of bodies onto the wagons.

The next day we heard how soldiers of both sides had broken into homes, demanding entrance, food, bed sheets for bandages. That wasn't bad enough.

They also demanded to stand on good carpets and smash perfectly good windows to fire their guns out of.

We heard that Mrs. French had muddy footprints all over her good ingrain carpet. That Mrs. Hose left her home on Baltimore Street. And when she got back the next day, her house was wrecked. Anna Howell Kennedy, over to West Washington Street, had a musket ball imbedded in the door of her carriage. People had horses stolen right out of their barns. A lot of women had clothing taken from their houses.

We were lucky, though the front window of Daddy's store had been smashed in and some goods taken. But the town wasn't ours yet, and Sky and I were still confined to our house and yard. I could hate the Rebels on that score alone. Then I remembered what Daddy had once said. That any time I wanted to hate somebody, I should make myself walk in their shoes for a while.

I tried it. I looked out the window. As it happened, a Reb soldier was just passing our house. I tried to imagine what it felt like walking in those high, dusty boots. Then I saw he was limping, dragging one foot, and the boot seemed to be cut and had bloodstains all over it. I was all ready to start forgiving him, or at least imagining his pain, when I heard Mama in the kitchen.

"Do you know that Rebel soldiers took three of Mrs. French's hoopskirts?" she was asking Aunt Lou. "Told her they wanted them for their womenfolk."

I peered out the window again to see the soldier all the way up the street, still limping. Good, I thought, I hope you limp all the way to Richmond.

The Rebels didn't leave us until Sunday, the twelfth, and, try as I could, I couldn't make myself walk even a block in their shoes. I thought if I didn't get away from our house soon, my skin would burst open. I wanted to see Josh. I wanted to ride Pillow. I wanted an ice cream.

Then, on that Sunday, Mama announced that we were going to church. "Rebels or no Rebels. It's Sunday," she announced, "and we belong in our place of worship. Let them try to stop us."

Then, just as Mama was coming down the stairs, we heard the guns.

"Oh, no!" she wailed.

Sky and I ran to the front door just in time to see shells flashing in the overcast sky on the outskirts of town. "That's where the Reb lines are, west and south of us," Sky said. "I'll bet it's our army, come to chase the Rebs away."

"Couldn't they wait until after church?" Mama asked. "Have they no respect?"

In the next few minutes, blue soldiers were charging through town. The church bells had just started to ring. Evangelical Lutheran, which was ours, St. John's Episcopal, and the Dutch Reformed — all at the same time.

We stood on the stoop for a minute. All up and down the street, we saw our neighbors doing the same thing. Standing, listening. No church in town rang its bells for that long of a Sunday. But it was as if all the ministers had decided, separate from one another, to keep right on ringing those bells. As if they knew the town folk had had enough of the guns. And this day they were going to offset the sound of war with God's music.

The church bells rang for an hour, as long as the gunshots lasted. When the bells stopped, we knew the battle was over. Then we went out into the street to see Rebels throwing down their arms. People were cheering, raising their arms in welcome. The men took off their hats. For what?

Then we looked. And saw.

A parade was coming through, a regular parade, with near a hundred men, walking, riding on prancing horses, doffing their hats, and everything. As they came closer, we could see they were ours. An officer was in the lead on a fine horse. The officer had long blond curls. He was nodding and waving to all the ladies. Young girls were running out into the street to meet him, throwing flowers, gloves, handkerchiefs at him. Behind him came a ragged group of men playing fifes and drums. Walking alongside the parade were other blue soldiers, their muskets aimed at the backs of ragged Rebels they'd rounded up, their prisoners.

"Who is it?" I asked Sky.

"Custer and his 1st Michigan."

"Why does he have long blond curls?"

"That's just the way Custer is," Sky answered.

We watched them parade for a while, watched Custer and his men accept the cheers, the thanks. I saw one young woman run right up to him with her arms thrown out. He bent down gallantly from his horse and kissed her.

"It's Lutie Kealhofer," I said.

"It can't be," Sky said, "she's a Rebel."

We proceeded on down the street, a little behind the parade, to church. Rebels were being ferreted out of alleys by blue soldiers and rounded up all around us. "I could have sworn it was Lutie Kealhofer," I said to Mama. "Doesn't matter if she's a Rebel. She's crazy over any officer in uniform."

Mama said it wasn't Christian, me saying that. And on a Sunday, too. So then I thought, all right. Maybe Lutie's decided to walk in Custer's boots for a while. And found that she liked them. But don't tell me it wasn't Lutie Kealhofer.

CHAPTER THIRTEEN

Josh's Big Story

FEBRUARY 1864

Sky wasn't even twelve yet, and he was getting more contentious every day, strutting about like a man in the new trousers and jacket he'd gotten for Christmas. It was a reward, Daddy said, for the way he'd filled a man's shoes when we had the battle in town, after Gettysburg.

"How did he fill a man's shoes?" I asked Daddy. "All he did was sit on the roof and look through your spyglass. I did that, too."

"Wasn't he ready to drive you, your mother, and Aunt Lou to Pennsylvania if the Confederates won?"

"It was my idea to go. To get Aunt Lou out of here."

I was helping him in the store, as I sometimes did. I liked those times, because it gave us a chance to talk without Sky, or anyone else, around. He was stacking some canned sardines. "Don't be envious of your brother, Amelia. He's at an age where he needs to feel important."

"Important? If he gets any more important he'll explode!" I was stacking some scented soap. Grandma Schuyler had managed to smuggle some to us for Daddy's best women customers. "He acts as if he's my superior," I complained. "He puts himself at a distance. Just because he reads the papers now, and you discuss issues of the day with him."

"I'll discuss issues of the day with you, too, Amelia, if you like."

I stared at him. Was he teasing? No, he was not. But I knew one thing, I'd better be prepared if I said yes. Because if I wasn't, he'd mark me down as a spoiled little piece, nothing more.

"I'd like that," I said.

"Very well," he said, mildly. "So, then. What do you think of the North using colored troops in the war?"

I thought a moment. "Well, Robert Moxley and his band were recruited last August, but I don't like the way the army is using them. They aren't fighting. They're just playing their music."

"They're being used to recruit more colored troops," Daddy said.

"I know that. But it's like the army isn't taking

them seriously. They want to fight. They've said that."

"Maybe what they're doing is more valuable to the army," he said. "Colored troops have already proved themselves at Fort Wagner."

I nodded, feeling warm and gratified. He was taking me seriously. "What do you think of General Meade?" I asked. "Do you think he was at fault by not pressing his advantage over Lee after Gettysburg?"

He smiled. "Some things about this war will take years to be figured out, Amelia. But I see you are reading the papers and observing. I didn't think you were that interested in this war."

"How could a person not be interested? I'm not a fliberty-gidget girl, Daddy."

"No. You aren't. Which makes it so puzzling to me why you refuse to engage in any of the activities to help in the war effort that your mother suggests to you."

I blushed. "They're silly, Daddy, all of them."

"Making a flag for the hospital is silly? Knitting for the soldiers is silly?"

"No. But the women sound so silly when they get together to do these things. They talk about such stupid things."

He finished stacking the canned sardines and stood up. "They all have men away at war, Amelia.

Sometimes sanity is maintained by talking about senseless, everyday things." He was frowning, angry with me now. I couldn't bear my father being angry with me. He seldom scolded, and maybe that was why. He was so dear.

"I think, if you don't mind my saying, Amelia, that you are still committed to not taking sides, after what happened the day Dewitt was shot," he said, walking to the end of the counter to straighten it. "I would hope you'd be over that childishness by now."

"It's just that when I do something, I want it to be important."

"We all can't be important, Amelia."

"Jinny Pearl is."

He raised an eyebrow. "Oh?"

"Uh-huh." He was watching me closely. I wanted him to know why I felt like I did. I didn't want him to think I was being a spoiled little piece. "If I tell you something, Daddy, do you promise to keep it secret?"

"Of course."

"Jinny Pearl ran off to join the army. As a man. She swore me to secrecy."

He sighed, and mused a moment. "Does Wes know?"

"I think so, yes. But you see what I mean now? When I do something, I want it to be important, too. I want you to think as much of me as you do of Sky."

He held his arms out to me, and I ran the length of the counter to hug him. "I love all my children the same, Amelia," he said.

"I know. But Sky is going to St. James College next year. You and Mama gave money to repair it so he could go! And I'm still going to Mrs. Winchester's day school. She thinks education is going to the Hagerstown Lyceum!"

He held me close. "It's the war, Amelia. Mrs. Winchester's is only until the Female Seminary opens again. I promise you. I don't think you're worth less because you're a girl."

I hugged him again. "I'll find something to do that is worthwhile," I promised.

"Fine, Amelia. Just don't go joining the army." He patted my head and reached for his coat. "Now let's get on home. Your mother is holding supper."

Now I had to find something worthwhile to do for the war. I'd promised Daddy. But I must be careful. It must be something that would mark me as intelligent and useful, yet not bring hurt down on anyone because of it.

I decided that I could start with Josh. He was itching to print another broadside, feeling the long, grinding days of February bearing down on him. He wanted to run his press again. But he had no newsprint. I would find him more wallpaper.

I asked Mrs. Winchester one day after school. She rustled up three rolls of old wallpaper which she had from her mother's house in Philadelphia. Josh was delighted with it. The plain side was good and strong for newsprint, he said. All he needed now was a good story.

Then I set out to find him a story. One that would not get his presses smashed. Josh still had Southern leanings, and the Union people were in power again, after Lee left Maryland in defeat after Gettysburg.

"Eight local ministers have signed a paper asking citizens to 'rise superior to the passions of the hour' by stopping acts of violence against those who rebelled against the Union," I told Josh one day. "Isn't that a story?"

"Not enough to waste my paper on."

When Wes came home unexpectedly on a short leave, the third week in February, I suggested that Josh interview him. So he invited Wes to the office. "I, along with ten thousand troops between Frederick and Harper's Ferry, weren't called on to assist at Gettysburg," Wes told him. "We were ready. Why weren't we called on? The war would be over by now."

Josh didn't print that story, either.

And then one day, when the weather was near zero, I was going to the bakery for Mama when there was a fuss on Potomac Street. Some blue soldiers had a man roped and were dragging him behind a horse on the frozen ground. The streets were near deserted, except for a man and a woman with packages in their arms, who stood watching. The poor man being dragged was yelling and begging to be released, as he skidded behind the horse over the jagged ice and dirt of the ground.

I went up to the elderly couple, whom I did not recognize. "Who is he?" I asked.

"Doctor Newall," the woman sobbed. "Oh, what a terrible act! Just because he supports the Southern cause! It isn't right, it isn't. Can't somebody stop them?"

"Come along, Mother," the man said. "There's nothing we can do about it. Nothing anybody can do."

I went on my way to the bakery, my footsteps ringing on the empty wooden sidewalk. *Nothing anybody can do.* I knew that was wrong. I was planning on stopping at the newspaper office after the bakery, to bring Josh some fresh buns.

By the time I purchased my bread and buns and walked to the newspaper office, I knew I wasn't going to tell Josh about Doctor Newall. He didn't need to print a story like that. It would raise his hackles against the Union soldiers. And he'd get his press smashed again. I said nothing. The elderly couple had been too frightened to tell anyone.

So I didn't tell him about the best story in a month. I kept silent.

I told him instead about Sergeant Carnes of Clear Spring, whose body was sent home on the train. Killed by Rebels.

"It's an obituary," he said, "not a story."

"He has a wife and six children. People are collecting money for them."

"I can't waste my newsprint on it."

"What are you waiting for, Abraham Lincoln to come through town?"

He just sat there drumming his fingers on the floor in front of him.

"Maybe you wouldn't even do a story then," I told him. "Maybe you'd wait for Jeff Davis."

He looked at me. "What are you saying?"

"That maybe you only want to do stories that favor the Confederacy."

"I'd do a story in a minute that favored the Union, if it was good," he said.

I thought about Doctor Newall, and flushed. "Well

then, you'll have to find it yourself, Josh. I'll not bring you another story."

"Nobody asked you to."

I stormed out. He made me so mad sometimes. Let him rot in that old newspaper office. He wouldn't see me for a while. I wasn't going to let him make a fool out of me.

We thought the cold couldn't get any worse, but it did. One bitter cold day, the last week in February, when nobody who had any brains would venture out, Mama started putting on her coat to take the new hospital flag she'd made to Doctor Lee at town hall. It was still being used for a hospital for wounded soldiers.

"I'll take it over." I jumped up from my chair by the fire in the parlor. "You shouldn't go out in this cold."

"Are you sure, Amelia?"

I said yes. Then she had a thought. "Why don't you bring it over to Josh and see if he wants to write about it?" she asked cheerfully. "It's a good story, and won't offend anyone. There are both Union and Rebel soldiers in the hospital. I'll send him some ham, bread, and cake."

I was fourteen and starting to realize that there was a certain innocence about Mama. And I didn't want to be the one to destroy it. So I said, all right, even though I knew Josh would laugh at the flag as a story idea. I bundled up good, took the food, and went to the barn to get Pillow. Together we ventured out onto the near-deserted streets. It had been a week since I'd seen Josh. I'd bring the food and never mention the flag. A mission of mercy.

Wind howled through town. The winter had been so cold that Daddy was using coal in the potbellied stove in the middle of his store. I decided, as the wind froze my breath and stung my nose, that this was foolish. I ought to go back home. And then I turned the corner and saw them.

A bunch of men, just standing there, a little around the corner from Andrew Hager's Feed Store. If you could call them men. I thought at first, given their ragged attire, their emaciated frames, that they were ghosts.

For a moment I just sat there on Pillow, clutching my cloak around me, and they stared.

They were Rebels, all right.

"Can I help you gentlemen?" I tried to sound cheerful, like Mama. But my voice cracked.

One stepped forward, over some puddles covered with ice. His boots were so worn down, his toes stuck out in front. He was dirty and unshaven. The uniform had an officer's bars on the tattered collar. But he had sores on his lips. His eyes were red-rimmed. Yet he took off his hat and bowed. "Miss? We don't know the layout of the town, but we know the Union army is in charge here. Can you tell us where headquarters is?" His Southern accent was thick.

"You're Rebs," I said. I was not frightened, but astonished. Where had they come from?

The officer allowed that they were.

"How did you get into town? We have Union pickets all over."

"We didn't see any pickets, miss. Fact is, we thought it peculiar-like that nobody was about."

"They're here," I said staunchly. The cold, I thought. Daddy had said he thought the pickets were taking refuge in the stores. He'd had two in his store yesterday. Still, didn't those stores have windows?

"You'd best be careful," I told them. "You're liable to get shot." I was not so sure of it, but I wanted to sound brave.

"We're not spoiling for a fight, miss," the officer said. "We have no guns."

"What do you want, then?"

"We're hungry," he admitted. "Fact is, we're about starved."

"Oh." I felt guilty with the basket of ham, bread, and cake tied in front of me. I wondered if they could smell it. I could. The ham was still warm.

"We want to surrender," the officer said. "If you

could just tell us where we could go so we could surrender."

I took them to Josh at the newspaper office. I knew I should have taken them to North Potomac Street, where the city hall and combined market house were headquarters to the Union army in town. But no soldiers were on the streets doing their job, and these men had come to me, hadn't they? I took them directly across the street to see Josh.

He gaped when he opened the door and saw them. "What in the sam hill?" he said.

"These men want to surrender, Josh," I said. "They're starving and cold. I brought them here. I have some bread and ham. Heaps of it. Mama sent it over. And if you want, I'll go home and fetch more. But I thought you'd like to talk to them first, maybe, and then take them to the proper authorities."

He let the soldiers in. The office was warm. They crowded in, fanning around the potbellied stove, holding out their hands to the heat. I introduced Josh. They shook his hand. They huddled around the coal stove and looked about to cry when I set down the basket, opened it, and handed around the ham and bread. They sank wearily on the floor and looked at the food in their hands, and thanked me profusely.

Josh always kept some food of his own around. He went out the back door to a box he kept there and brought in some cider. He had some dried apples, too, and some crackers. A feast.

Josh sat right down on the floor with them and started asking them things. Told them he wanted a story that would make everyone sick of the war. And they looked like they could tell it.

They did. They told him about how they'd been here in Hagerstown Seminary Hospital until last August, after Gettysburg. That they'd been exchanged as prisoners shortly after. But that they'd been captured again, and escaped last October from Fort Delaware, where smallpox had broken out and so many were dying.

All winter they'd been hiding, starving, freezing. Once they'd eaten rats. They could stand no more. They were deserting.

Josh and I listened to them for an hour. Then I went to fetch my father in the store. Because he was a town official. And he could see that they properly surrendered.

The next day Josh had his broadsides printed, telling the story of the prisoners. Daddy put a stack of them on the white pine counter in his store.

By the end of the week, when I visited Josh, I knew the reason for his long face.

"Nobody cares," he said. "Nobody gives a possum's tail about the story."

"Of course they care," I argued. "The women from our church brought them food and cleaned and mended their uniforms."

"How many broadsides did your father sell?"

I flushed. "Four."

"The other stores sold less. It just wasn't a good story. People are sick of the war. They don't care anymore. They're struggling and tired of it."

"It was a good story, Josh."

He looked at me with narrowed eyes. "The one about Doctor Newall would have been better."

I said nothing. So he'd found out. I just glared at him.

"I'd have printed that one. And people would have cared. Why didn't you tell me about it?"

"I didn't think it was so good," I hedged.

"You should have let me be the judge of that. A good doctor dragged through town by a horse because he had Southern sympathies? You didn't give it to me on purpose, Amelia. I know how your mind works."

We'd been sitting on the floor, eating. I stood up. "Oh, do you? Well, then, why don't you tell me how my mind works. Because I'm not so sure sometimes myself."

"Don't use me," he said.

"Use you?" I couldn't believe it!

"If you want to do something for the war, don't hide behind me. Take a risk and do it yourself."

"How am I hiding behind you?"

"By finding me stories. But only ones that won't get the town folk angry with me. You're playing it nice and safe, Amelia. It doesn't work that way. You can't be safe and do something worthwhile. You have to take chances."

"I never heard such folderol in my whole life, Josh Dechart! Don't you blame me because your broadsides didn't sell!"

He grinned. "Yeah, well, looks like we're both fooling ourselves, aren't we?"

Again I slammed out. "I'll never come back here," I vowed, "never. He can starve for all I care!" The wind howled around me as I rushed home. It froze the tears on my face.

The Rebels who'd surrendered were sent back to a Federal prison. Nothing was fair, I decided, nothing.

CHAPTER FOURTEEN

For Once They Named a Battle Right

MAY 1864

I didn't see Josh for a while after that. Part of it was that I was ashamed of holding back the story about Doctor Newall. Nobody needs people reminding them to be ashamed. So I stayed away, always intending to go, but never going. Since I made myself busy every time Mama suggested I bring him food, Sky did it. I had other things to worry about, didn't I? For one, I had to ride over to the Beale farm every so often to visit and to try to find out if Mrs. Beale had heard anything from Jinny Pearl.

When Wes came home in February, I'd promised him I'd do this. In a burst of brotherly trust, or need, he'd confided in me about Jinny's running off to be a soldier. I was so flattered at his confidence that I promised him I'd ride over to the Beale place at least once a month and see if anybody had heard anything about Jinny. Nobody had. Or if they had, they weren't telling anybody. Not me, anyway. But I kept my promise to Wes.

"You don't know what it's like, not knowing," Wes had said.

In May I knew. At least secondhand. Because by May we hadn't heard from Wes in six weeks, and I couldn't stand the anguish it caused Mama. Wes wrote at least once a month. The letters came to us in envelopes that were smudged and torn. Sometimes they were written on anything but proper paper. Sometimes I thought they were downright stupid. Once, in February, he wrote from Washington how six horses and ponies died in a fire in the White House stables, and President Lincoln himself tried to get them out. That's when he was doing picket duty in front of the White House. I thought he was being pompous, bragging. Mama didn't. She hung onto every word of that letter, like she cared that it wasn't as cold down there as it was here, that the streets didn't freeze and the rain turned them to mud.

She acted like she knew who O. O. Howard's 11th Corps was. She felt bad for them, a corps of German immigrant boys who everybody called Ugly Ducklings. And when Wes wrote, "Has anybody heard from Jinny Pearl? Has Amelia been to the Beale place like she promised?" — she sent me over that day.

Right after she sent Sky to Daddy's store for a good pair of gloves, suspender buckles, needles, pins, thread, and some jawbreakers to send to Wes. She kept Wes's letters in a blue box in her bedroom. When the box opened, it played music. Some waltz. It was very precious to her.

But it was six weeks now since she'd heard from Wes. And she just knew he was dead. She just knew it, she confided in me.

It was the morning of the day we heard about the battle they called The Wilderness. Word came on the telegraph that it was the biggest battle yet this year. The newspapers said there were over seven thousand Rebel casualties. And our army had over seventeen thousand.

Every day, Daddy went to the telegraph office to look at the names of the missing and dead. Then he'd send home a note telling Mama Wes wasn't on it. We didn't even know if Wes had been in the battle. At first we didn't even know where this place called The Wilderness was. (It was in Virginia.)

And then, one day, Doctor John McKinnow came up our walk and knocked on our front door. Everybody knew that Doctor McKinnow had been selected by the county commissioners to go to Virginia and aid in the treatment of the men from Washington County who'd been wounded in The Wilderness.

Mama was at the breakfast table, writing to Grandmother Schuyler. Daddy had left for the store. Sky for school. I was gathering my things to leave for school. Aunt Lou was out back, hanging the bed linen on the drying line.

"Go see who's at the door, Amelia," Mama directed.

I went. "It's Doctor McKinnow," I said.

And that's when Mama fainted.

"I tol' her and tol' her," Aunt Lou said to Doctor McKinnow, "that she should rest afternoons. But she won't listen. Still goes to that hospital every day and nurses those soldiers. A woman in her condition."

Mama was on the settee in the parlor. Doctor McKinnow had just checked her to make sure she was all right. Aunt Lou was scolding. Mama was sitting up, flustered and embarrassed. "I'm perfectly able to go to the hospital, Aunt Lou. Aren't I, Doctor?"

He shook his head. "You could contract any number of diseases," he admonished gently. "I'd say no, Mrs. Grafton. Not until you come to the end of your confinement."

I stood in the hall, dazed. Mama was going to have a baby! How could that be? But then, of course, I knew how it could be. Mama was still a young woman, not yet forty. But think of it! A baby! Why hadn't anybody told me?

"I fainted because I thought Wes was dead," Mama was telling the doctor and Aunt Lou.

"He isn't dead, Mrs. Grafton," the doctor told her. "Just wounded. In the arm. No bones hit, from what I've heard. But infection must be staved off. The army doctors down there cannot handle all the wounded, so, as you know, I've been commissioned to go and treat the boys from Washington County. I stopped by to see what you want to send along with me to Wes."

Mama was so grateful Wes was alive that she almost hugged Doctor McKinnow. "Amelia," she called out to me, "bring me my writing things. I must pen a note to Wes immediately. Aunt Lou, go upstairs and get together some clean shirts and socks. Some of his favorite books. And see if there are any jawbreakers left in the kitchen."

I fetched her writing things and set up a small table for her in the parlor. I stared at her as she set herself to the task of writing. A baby! She didn't look it. She hadn't gained any weight yet. I wondered if she'd tell Wes.

"Amelia, don't just stand there," she said. "Fetch a plate of breakfast and some hot coffee for the doctor in the dining room. Doctor, do go to the dining room.

I'll have this note penned in a jiffy. I know your time is precious."

She had the whole house scurrying to do her bidding. Even Doctor McKinnow. He obeyed, and took a place at the dining room table. I heaped a plate full of grits, ham, and eggs left from breakfast. I filled his cup with coffee, then sat down to watch him eat.

"Won't you be late for school, Amelia?" he asked.

"Yes, but I don't care. I don't learn much at Mrs. Winchester's."

"It's too bad the seminary is still closed. You belong there."

"Doctor, can I ask you a question?"

"Your brother will be all right, don't worry. He won't be sent to a prison camp. Likely, though, he will be returned to duty when he heals."

"It isn't about Wes. It's about my mother. Is she really to have a baby?"

"I'm not her doctor, Amelia. But if Aunt Lou says so, I'm sure it is. And fainting is nothing to worry about. Many women who are expecting a child faint."

"Well, I didn't know it, is all. Nobody told me."

He smiled. "I'm sure your parents were about to. Your mother told me she is at the beginning of her confinement. Many times women don't like to tell anybody until they get past the first couple of months

194

and are sure everything will be all right. You're old enough to understand that, aren't you?"

"Yessir. Now, can I ask you another question?"

"Go ahead, Amelia. But the stork doesn't bring babies. You're old enough to know that."

"I know that." I blushed. "What I need to know doesn't have to do with Mama."

"Well, go ahead, then."

"If you were treating a wounded soldier and you found out it was a girl, what would you do?"

"Not thinking of joining the army, are you?"

"No, but girls do."

"You are right. Women have run off to join the army."

"If they get wounded, do doctors give them away?"

"If they're in the military they do. Fact is, I heard tell about a woman named Annie Lillybridge. From Detroit. She served in the 21st Michigan Infantry. At the battle of Pea Ridge in Arkansas in '62, she was wounded in the arm. A surgeon discovered she was a woman, and turned her in. She was given a discharge out of the army, but she swapped it with another soldier and re-enlisted. If women really want to fight, Amelia, they'll find a way."

I nodded solemnly.

"Do you know somebody who's thinking of joining?" he asked gently.

"No, sir. I just got to thinking about it."

He was eyeing me narrowly, as if he didn't believe me.

"Do you know of anyone?" I asked innocently.

He delicately picked up the last of the ham with his fork. "I might."

"Who? Is she from Washington County?"

"We doctors hear all kinds of things, Amelia. I couldn't tell you if I wanted to. It would go against my calling."

I nodded thoughtfully. "People can tell you all kinds of things, and you have to keep it secret, then?"

"That's what it means, Amelia."

"I hate keeping people's secrets. Most secrets aren't nice. But once you promise to, you have to keep them, don't you?"

"The trick is not to promise. But then, at your age, what secrets could be so bad?"

You should know about the dead Rebel soldier on the Beale place, I thought. Then I gave the conversation a new turn. "Why do they call it The Wilderness, where Wes was wounded?"

"The place where they fought is overgrown, the underbrush so dense, it can cut a man up or entangle him. The roads are bad. The Confederate army had the advantage because they were accustomed to that countryside. Then the woods caught fire and many of the wounded were stranded and couldn't get out."

"How did Wes get out?"

"Some did. The lucky ones."

I stood up. "Do you think you have room in that package for some sugar cookies for Wes?"

"I think Wes would love some sugar cookies from home."

For once they named a battle right, I decided. I went to get the cookies, hearing the screams of the men who couldn't get out of those burning woods, inside my head.

CHAPTER FIFTEEN

A Rock Through the Window

JULY 1864

The morning was hot already at seven-thirty when the rock came through the dining room window. The rock did its job. It sent splinters of jagged glass all around, and set Mama to screaming. Mama never screamed. But the sound of that rock, the sound of that glass was like an explosion. It not only broke the peace of our breakfast that Saturday morning, it broke the peace of our house. And it changed everything.

Things had been pretty quiet, considering that we never knew, day to day, hour to hour, which army was occupying our town. Since the first day of July, there had been fighting on our streets, guns going off, cavalry galloping through, just to show how fast their horses could gallop, it seemed, people either bolting themselves inside their houses, or leaving. It was now the sixth day of July. When the rock came, Daddy was just saying how perfect the roses were in the vase on the sideboard. Mama had just said that it was a year since Gettysburg, and how the last of the wounded had just been shipped out of our hospital at the end of May.

We were having one of those moments when we were pretending there was no war out on our streets. Sometimes we could do that in our house. Sit and talk about things like we used to do, at a table covered with a crisp white cloth and silverware and good food. The only thing missing was Mama's silver tea service. Mama never talked about it. And we hadn't heard from Aunt Charlotte since that day she carted it off in the laundry basket.

I was thinking how nice a breakfast it was, and wondering how many other families were pretending there was no war, too, when the rock came with its sound as loud as cannister shot. Sky jumped up. Daddy held him back by the arm and we all just stared, openmouthed.

A note was tied around it with a string. I thought Aunt Lou was going to drop the platter of pancakes she was holding as she came in from the kitchen.

Mama stood holding her linen napkin in front of

her mouth and shaking. "It's all right," Daddy said, "it's all right, Leigh. It's just a rock. No, don't touch it, Sky, there's too much glass around. Aunt Lou, would you get a broom, please?"

His calm voice made sense out of chaos. I stood staring at the glass. It sparkled like diamonds in the flood of morning sun. The rock seemed so out of place on the floor. So *obscene*. Yes, there was a war out on the streets, but you didn't go thrusting it into someone's house like that. There were rules. Even in war. Daddy picked up the rock, untied the note, and read it.

"What does it say?" from Mama, who had become calmed herself somewhat. "Who is it from?"

Daddy knelt there with the note in his hand and looked up at her, and smiled. "Probably some nettled local who is put out because we have eggs on the table and they haven't."

"But what does it *say*?" Mama persisted.

Daddy stood up. "'People who have the best provisions on their table, when others do without, should be ashamed.'"

"Oh, dear," Mama said. Then, "It doesn't come from the Confederates, I know that."

"Leigh," Daddy said, "have you been trading again?"

A look passed between them. Sky and I just stared. Mama nodded. "Well, yes, Wes, how could I not? The officer who knocked on the back door last night needed some bacon. He was offering coffee and sugar. We needed that, so I made the trade."

Daddy nodded and looked down at the note in his hand. "No, it doesn't come from the Confederates. I'm sure it comes from one of our neighbors, who nods and smiles at us on the street every day. I think it's time I made a run to Pennsylvania and brought back some coffee and other essentials. I'll go tonight."

"Wes, you can't go now. You'll be waylaid on the trip. There are bands of starving soldiers roaming the countryside." Mama almost wailed it, and Mama never wailed.

"Now, now, Leigh, I know the way. I've made the trip dozens of times. I must think of my family. I didn't know we were in need of anything. And what of my customers? They ask me, daily, for molasses, coffee, calico. Pack my things, Leigh. And don't worry. Sky, get to work and finish painting that fence today." He turned to leave. "I'll see what I can bring home to put on the window. I'm afraid a pane of glass is out of the question right now." He turned to leave.

"Don't make sense, painting a fence with the Rebels here again," Sky declared.

The fence that outlined our property was in disrepair from two summers of armies coming through. We were lucky to have it at all. All over the county, fences were down. Both armies had used them for wood.

"Don't argue, Sky. I want the fence painted." Daddy left.

Aunt Lou came in and swept up the glass, then drew the summer drapes over the broken window. I wished they would flutter, but there was no breeze. We finished our breakfast, and then I went upstairs to help Mama pack Daddy's things.

"Mama, how long have you been trading with the Confederates?" I asked.

She started taking shirts out of Daddy's wardrobe. "I have done it on occasion, Amelia. I know they are the enemy, but I try to imagine Wes out there someplace, in need of bacon. And when I do, I hope some Southern lady is kind enough to exchange food with him. Now, I do not wish to speak of it. And I do not wish you to speak of it. To anyone. Fetch your father's shaving mug and razor. Please."

I went to do her bidding. Imagine! My mother answering a knock on the door late at night and trading food with the enemy! I looked at her differently, after that. You never could tell, I decided. Never. Especially with Mama.

I thought it was very exciting. I wondered what the Confederate officer had looked like who'd come to the door. Had they spoken? Or done the exchange in silence?

We packed Daddy's things. Sky came upstairs and stood in the doorway. His britches were full of white paint. He signaled me, and I slipped out into the hall.

"McLean's got his men on the south end of town," he whispered.

I stared at him. Was I supposed to understand what this meant? Sky kept up with all the officers' names on both sides of the war. I didn't. Oh, I'd heard all the names, but they played themselves out in minor notes on the background of my everyday existence.

"McLean is ours," Sky explained. "He's up against Shearer, from the 1st Maryland Reb Cavalry. I heard that Shearer is the vanguard of McCausland's forces."

McCausland? I stared at Sky. That name I knew. "Where is McCausland?"

"They say he's on his way here. Why?"

My face went white. "I know who McCausland is."

"He's a Southern general. I just told you."

"No, he's more than that. McCausland is Josh Dechart's uncle. His mother's brother."

"I thought you didn't care about Josh anymore. You haven't spoken to him all spring."

"It isn't Josh I'm thinking of. It's Mama." I looked at Sky. "McCausland is not a man of good parts, from what I've heard. If he aims to occupy our town, we should leave. Get Mama out. You know her condition, Sky."

He nodded solemnly. "What'd you hear about McCausland?"

"Josh always bragged about him. How he was only seven when both his parents died. How they were Irish immigrants. How he graduated Virginia Military Institute at the top of his class. How he gave a good account of himself in Virginia. McCausland didn't get that way by being nice, Sky."

"Mama's given food to Confederates," he whispered, pulling me farther into the hall. "They wouldn't hurt her."

For all his knowledge of the generals and their movements, Sky was still a child. I could see that. "We should try to see Josh, Sky. This morning. Likely he'll know what his uncle is up to. He may even have been to see him already. We should know, before Daddy leaves tonight, what McCausland intends about our town! And if we should all leave with Daddy."

Before he could answer, Mama came out of the bedroom into the hall. "What's going on, you two?"

"Mama, can we go to town?" I asked. "I'd like to bring Josh some food."

Her eyebrows went up. "You haven't spoken to him in months, Amelia. I had to have Sky bring it. Why the sudden change of heart?"

I shrugged. "After what you've been doing, giving food to Confederates, I thought it was selfish of me to ignore Josh anymore, Mama. I feel guilty. I'd like to bring a basket this morning. Please?"

She frowned, taking my measure. I did my best to look innocent. "Oh, all right, ask Aunt Lou to pack a basket for him. Sky, you go with her, and if there's any sign of trouble, come home immediately, you hear?"

"Yes, Mama."

"And ask Aunt Lou to bring up some coffee and a powder. I'm getting one of my headaches, and I must lie down."

Sky and I went downstairs. On the landing, he paused and looked at me. "They've got martial law in Chambersburg, Pennsylvania," he said.

"What's that?"

"It's when the army takes over. It's in charge. Daddy read it in the *Baltimore American* yesterday."

"I can't imagine the army in charge of anything. Theirs or ours. All we ever have when they're in charge are lootings, shootings, and mayhem."

"The people can't go outside town limits without a pass," Sky went on. "Sometimes they can't even walk on the streets without a good reason. And if they're caught without a pass, they're taken into the woods, miles away, and left, abandoned!"

"Who does this?"

"Both sides, when there's martial law," he said importantly. "But we don't have that here. We can come and go as we please. Aren't we lucky?"

I nodded. "I'll tell Aunt Lou to bring up the coffee and headache powder. Then I'll fetch some food for Josh."

He nodded. "I'll met you in the front yard," he said.

What would I say to Josh, after months of ignoring him, I wondered, as I arranged some food in a basket. Of a sudden, I saw his face before me, the freckles, the brown eyes, the specs, the lean determination. Somehow I sensed it didn't matter that we hadn't spoken in so long, that our friendship went beyond that. The urgency of the moment would get us through.

As I passed through the front hallway, I saw the

roses on the sideboard, still pretty. If anybody had said to me when I woke this morning that I'd be rushing off to see Josh Dechart with food today I'd have called them crazy. So much had changed when that rock came through the window. So much in one hour.

CHAPTER SIXTEEN

He's a Reb,
Through and Through

On the way, Sky and I plotted. We would tell Josh that we were coming to bring him the news Sky had heard the soldiers talking of while he was out front painting the fence this morning — that McCausland was coming. And we wouldn't tell Mama or Daddy we might have to leave tonight until we were sure.

I felt more than a little guilty, plotting against my old friend. But then, I consoled myself with the thought that maybe we *were* bringing this news. Maybe he didn't know yet.

When Josh opened the door he said, "Hey, Sky." But he was looking at me as he said it. I got no hey. Just a nod. He seemed older. Taller. And grimmer. His clothes were clean, but the shirt had seen better days, and the cuffs were too short. His red hair needed cutting.

"Hey, Josh," I said.

"What are you doing here?"

"Well, if you're going to be that way, I can leave."

"Who said anything about leaving? I'm just asking."

"I thought it was time to end our silly argument. I've got food. And news."

He looked at the basket in my hand. "I can smell the food. And the news, too. It's bad, isn't it?"

"For us, maybe. But not for you."

He scowled. "You gonna start, Amelia? That what you've come for?"

I smiled sweetly. "No, I told you. I thought it time to end our silly argument. I've been ashamed for not coming to see you all these months. Only, I didn't know what excuse to make for coming."

"You don't need an excuse," he said.

My spirits lifted. So our friendship had held. "Anyway, I have one. I came to tell you that Shearer is coming. The 1st Maryland Cavalry. And he's the vanguard of your uncle's forces." I sounded older, and important, saying it.

Josh only nodded and reached again for the basket. "You going to give me the food?"

"Your uncle is coming, Josh!" I repeated.

"I know."

I felt the wind go out of my sails. "How?" I held out the basket.

"I have my sources."

I thought that was high-toned. And rude. He took the basket and grabbed an apple out of it, and started eating. "Look at that," he pointed to a newspaper, the *Washington Star*. "It says the military action here is only a bogus Harrisburg report. I hate it when newspapers can't get things right. Here I am holding on to whatever little wallpaper I have left so I can print the truth, and these big-city papers can't get the truth when it stares them in the face. Do they think a Southern general would be on the outskirts of Hagerstown if it were bogus?"

"Why is your uncle coming, Josh?" I asked.

"I don't know. But I hope to find out. I'm going out to meet him this morning."

"Are they going to occupy our town?"

"I aim to write the story soon's I get back. I imagine he'll have a lot to tell me."

"Will you tell us first?"

He was reaching for some sliced ham and a biscuit. He dropped both like he'd just found they were covered with fire ants. "I can't do that, Amelia," he said.

I could see, right off, that he saw the food as a bribe. He'd starve first. I knew him that well. "Josh," I said, "we have to know. Before tonight. Because my daddy is leaving tonight. My mama's having a baby. If your uncle is going to invade, might be we should get our mama away."

He considered that. "I'm glad for your mama," he said huskily. "But I can't do that, Amelia. When I interview somebody, when I ask them to tell me the truth, and to trust me, I can't go giving away that information to people who need to know it for their own reasons."

I couldn't believe it. "Not even when those people are your friends who may be in trouble?"

"No. Not even then," he said.

"Didn't you hear what I said?" I stared up at him. "My mama is having a baby! We need this information, Josh. We're your friends. Didn't my mama and daddy always send food around to you? Didn't I get you wallpaper to print on?"

He picked up the basket and thrust it back at me. "Where have you been since February, Amelia?" he asked. "I don't want your friendship, or your food, if I'm asked to compromise myself."

I took the basket. He reached for his jacket. "I'm sorry, Amelia. Anyway, my uncle isn't a monster. He doesn't raid women and children or turn them out of their houses. Your mother will be fine if she stays." He looked at me.

I looked down at the floor. "Fine," I said.

"I've got to go now. The judge gave me loan of a horse. It's out back. I'm riding to my uncle's camp. Lock the door when you leave."

"We'll leave now," I said. My voice was tight. I could scarce speak. I nodded to Sky, and he followed me out back. We stood there watching. And waiting for him to leave. But he didn't leave right off. He just sat there on that horse, looking at us.

"I'm sorry," he said. "I don't want to hurt you, Amelia. We've been good friends."

"Well, we won't be anymore if you don't stop by the house on your way home and tell us what to expect," I told him.

"Everybody has to do what they have to do," he said.

"Right."

"You've changed, Amelia."

"So have you." My heart was hammering inside me. I felt the end of things between us. "If you don't let us know soon's you hear, I think it's time we started putting some daylight between us."

He nodded and pressed his heels into the horse's flanks. Then he rode off.

"He won't come," Sky said. "He's a Reb, through and through."

"I should have known," I said.

"Well, he had me fooled," Sky said. "We've been feeding a Reb all this time."

"We've fed others," I told him.

"But he had me fooled," Sky said.

He had me fooled, too, I thought, as we started walking home. Only I didn't say it.

CHAPTER SEVENTEEN

Everybody Does What
They Have to Do

When we got home, I went inside. Aunt Lou said Mama was still lying down with her headache and I wasn't to make any noise. I had no intention of making any noise, and I resented being treated like a child. So I went up to my room and tried writing a letter to Wes. The last we'd heard from him he was still in Virginia, recovering from his wound. Doctor McKinnow had managed to stave off infection and Wes's arm was healing nicely. He might soon be returned to duty.

I wondered if I should tell him that we might all leave tonight, then decided against it. Josh could still come and say we didn't have to. I put down my pen and gazed out the window. Josh might think over what I had said and still come to warn us. And he might not like what he saw or heard when he got to his uncle's camp.

Was I a fool for thinking this? Do we think what we want to think, hoping it will be true? Suppose Wes got a furlough and came home, and we weren't there? That was unlikely, I decided. Then I wondered, which is more unlikely — Wes getting a furlough, or Josh being a friend and coming to tell us what his uncle had planned for Hagerstown?

Oh, I had a headache! I couldn't decide. And then I heard Daddy come in downstairs, heard him come up the stairs and go to their room and speak to Mama in low tones. I went out into the hall to listen.

"Now Leigh, don't worry, everything is quiet in town. There's no real news this morning. Do you feel up to coming down and joining us at the table?"

He didn't know about McCausland! Or he was lying to Mama. No, I decided, he wouldn't lie. He'd come home, if he knew, and tell her we had to leave, that it was best. My daddy was nothing if not honest with all of us all the time.

I went back to my room. In a little while, he knocked, opened the door, and came in smiling. "Coming down to eat, Amelia?"

He wasn't hiding anything. I could tell by the look on his face. I said yes and followed him down the stairs. He didn't know about McCausland. And Sky and I would wait just a little longer. Just in case Josh thought it over and decided to be a friend and tell us there was nothing to worry about.

I hated the idea of packing to leave. Because Daddy had told us once that if and when we had to leave, we'd be war refugees, just like all those people I'd always seen leaving town every time the Rebels came, with their possessions all in one bag, or piled in a wagon. War refugees didn't take all they held dear. They took only one bag, Daddy had said. I couldn't stand the idea of leaving any of my things behind. That's why I hated it.

But that afternoon, when Mama went back to her room to lie down, because she still had a headache, and Sky went out to finish painting the fence, I made myself pack. I did it as a talisman. If I went through the trouble, I'd end up having not to go.

I took only one dress and change of underwear. Grandmother Schuyler would have clothes for me. Or get me some. Instead of clothes, I packed my favorite books, my old doll from my childhood, some toilette items, a daguerreotype of Mama and Daddy, some precious writing paper, and my silver-backed hairbrush.

I rearranged it all about ten times, then stood back,

satisfied. "There, Josh," I said to myself, "I'm ready to leave, with my mama. Now let's see what you're ready to do about it."

The house was so quiet. I picked up a book and sat down on the window seat to read. After about an hour, I heard someone coming softly up the stairs. I waited. The door of my room was open, and in a minute, Sky stood there in his paint-splotched trousers.

His face looked funny, the way it had looked when he'd come back from the battlefield that time with his loot. Like he'd seen something he'd never seen before, never expected to see, and was really taken with it. "Amelia," he said quietly, "Josh is outside. He's here to see you."

His horse was by the water trough in front. He stood under the linden tree in the backyard. He looked dusty, and the sweatband of his hat was full of sweat. "Hey, Amelia," he said.

"You came back."

He nodded. He had something in his hand, a folded piece of paper. I looked at it, then at him.

"Did you see your uncle?"

"Oh, I saw him, all right."

It was bad, then. Worse than I'd thought. "Do we have to leave? Should we pack?"

He shook his head no and looked down at the paper in his hand. "You can't," he said. "Your daddy will be needed here. He's the only town official who hasn't left, isn't he?"

"I don't know." My lips were dry. Katydids were screaming in the background, their drone growing and growing in pitch. It was getting hotter by the minute.

Josh nodded. "Last I heard, your daddy was the only official left in town. So you all can't leave. He's gonna be needed."

I nodded. Something here was just out of reach of my understanding. "Why is he going to be needed, Josh?"

He looked at me, and I saw sadness in his eyes that I hadn't known he had in him. "My uncle wants two hundred thousand dollars or he's gonna burn the town," he said.

I didn't understand. The words did not connect inside me with anything. Words have to have some range of experience in your mind to connect to. I had never heard of anybody wanting to burn a whole town. Then I looked into Josh's eyes again, and saw that it was true.

"I wish I hadn't gone, Amelia. He wouldn't let me interview him. When I got there, he saw me as the one to bring the message. I swear, Amelia, I'd never have gone if I'd known what would come of it."

This was more than I could abide. "Is that it? In your hand? The message?"

"He also wants any government stores the town has," he said. "And he wants shirts, britches, hats, shoes, socks for all his men. They are in dire need."

"How many men does he have?"

"Fifteen hundred."

I laughed. "We don't have such things! Why do you think my daddy is planning a trip to Pennsylvania! To get things for his customers."

"Whatever we've got he wants. Plus the money. He's dead serious, Amelia."

I reached out my hand for the paper. "Let me see the order, Josh."

"I could get in trouble showing this to anybody. By rights, I'm not supposed to look at it myself, except that he dictated it to his aide right in front of me. And had the aide hand it right to me, after."

"It's what you came for, isn't it? To show it to us?"

He nodded and handed it to me. "It isn't my uncle's idea. He's following the orders of General Jubal Early. My uncle just made me the courier. I'm to bring it to an official, and tell him that my uncle and his men should be here soon."

I read it.

HEADQUARTERS, CAVALRY BRIGADE
HAGERSTOWN, MD. JULY 6TH 1864

*In accordance with the instruction of Lt. Gen.
Early, a levy of $200,000 is made upon the in-
habitants of this city. The space of three hours is
allowed for the payment of this sum in U.S. funds.*

*A requisition is also made for all government
stores. The following articles will also be fur-
nished, from the merchandise now in the hands of
the citizens or merchants, viz: 1500 shirts, 1500
suits of clothing, 1500 hats, 1500 pairs of shoes or
boots, 1900 pairs of drawers, and 1500 pairs of
socks. Four hours will be allowed for this collection.*

*The mayor and council are held responsible for
the execution of this order, and in case of non-
compliance the usual penalty will be enforced
upon the city.*

JOHN MCCAUSLAND,
BRIGADIER GENERAL C.S.A.

A little behind Josh, Duke and Duchess were
sprawled out under some bushes, sleeping. Everything was so quiet and peaceful here. Birds sang in

the trees. The sun was slanting in the west. When it went down, it was going to be a pleasant evening. How could all this be real?

"He's a brigadier general now," Josh said. "I felt I owed you something. I was wrong about things. And your daddy's been so good to me."

"My daddy is a decent man, Josh. This is going to kill him."

"So what do you think we should do, then?"

"Bring it to him. He'd never forgive us if we didn't. But we have to think first."

"About what?"

"What we can do about it. If we can do anything."

They looked at me — Josh and Sky — like I was daft. "How can you do anything about a general order but deliver it?" Sky asked.

"I don't know," I said, "but we should think about it first, shouldn't we? Just in case there's something we can do?"

Josh shrugged. "I just came to show it to you. Like I said, I owed you that, Amelia."

"Sky, why don't you take Josh into the kitchen and give him some lemonade and let him wash up," I said. "Aunt Lou has gone out on an errand. Give me some time."

Josh reached for the note, but I held it back, saying I just wanted to study it. I watched them walk across

221

the grass to the side entrance of the house. "Maybe you could say you lost the order," Sky was saying, "the way order number 191 was lost at Antietam two years ago. And found by a Yankee private. Remember? It was wrapped around three cigars. When the Yankee private brought it to his superiors — well, that's why Lee lost at Antietam."

Sky with his stories! I sat down under the linden tree to think. I felt the desolation settle over me. I had to pray, that's what I had to do. Please God, send me a thought. There was a thought, whirling around in my mind. But it was escaping me. It had something to do with something Sky had just said.

Something about the general order being lost at Antietam.

I knew we couldn't pretend Josh had lost the order. We couldn't put the blame of it on him. It wouldn't be right. What, then?

It came to me. Clear as a bell in the night it came to me. Like the heavens opened up and God spoke to me. Like some religious rapture they talk about. I know it sounded crazy. God had enough on His mind right then, what with President Lincoln suspending the writ of habeas corpus and proclaiming martial law in Kentucky. And everyone thinking Washington would be captured by the Confederates. God didn't speak to little girls in Hagerstown, Maryland.

But He spoke to me just then, I knew it. Clear as if He'd said, "The candy, Amelia. Remember the note with the candy."

"I know," I said softly. "I know." And I opened the order and looked at it again.

There it was. $200,000. In figures.

But how? How would I do it? With what? And could I do it before they came out of the house? Because I knew I had to do it myself. Not tell them.

But what would happen when my daddy gave the order back to McCausland, and he saw it asked for only $20,000 instead of $200,000? Well, if God was with us, McCausland would think that the aide had had a slip of the pen in the writing. Hadn't Josh said an aide had written it? And handed it right to him?

Then McCausland hadn't seen it. There could be a mistake on it!

I felt a thrill come over me. My daddy was town treasurer. I knew we could afford $20,000. I also knew that if it was $200,000, the town would burn. I didn't care for myself. I never liked this place, anyway, I told myself. I'm doing it for Mama and Daddy, and all the other people who have been through so much since this fool war started.

I knew the lie of that, even as I said it. I cared about our house, didn't I? I'd die if it was burned. And other people cared about their houses, too, didn't they? That's what a town was — everybody's individual house. And church. And store.

Besides, why should some Rebel general be allowed to burn it? Why should they be allowed to punish civilians? I got downright taken with the rightness and the fitness of it.

But how would I do it? What would I use? The order was in ink.

My heart sank. There was no way to do it. So what good was the rightness of it, if you couldn't do it? I sat with my chin in my hand, looking around our yard. And then I saw it.

The bucket of paint Sky had left, with the brush sitting on top of it. I got up and looked to the house to see if anyone was in sight. No one was. I walked across the grass to the paint and picked up the brush. It was thick with the white paint. If I could just use the end of it, I thought, just separate two brush hairs. I spread the order out on the ground and separated two paint brush hairs from the rest. Carefully, I applied them to the zero on the end of the $200,000.

No! The comma was now in the wrong place! An aide to a general couldn't be that stupid!

What to do now? I felt panic, like bile, sour and rising in my throat. I needed to get out that comma and put it back in after the first zero, then place the third zero where the comma had been.

So I started with the two hairs of the paintbrush again and went over the last three zeros and the comma. Now it said $20 and there was a space where the zeros had been.

A space for me to put in a comma and three more zeros.

But ink. I needed pen and ink. Quickly, I ran around to the front of the house, opened the door, and listened. Josh and Sky were in the kitchen, talking and saying how good the cookies were. I tiptoed in, closed the door quietly behind me, and went into the front parlor, where there was pen and ink on Mama's desk.

I set the note down on the desk. My heart was hammering. My hands were sweating. But I had to go through with it now. I opened the ink bottle and dipped the pen in.

Was the white paint I'd just applied dry? Yes it was. Carefully, so carefully, I drew in the comma and the three more zeros. Then I studied my work.

You could scarce see the white paint, I'd applied it so carefully. There was a slight smudge. It looked like somebody had made a mistake and corrected it. And it said $20,000.

Quickly, I covered the ink and crept out the front

of the house and around the yard, waving the order so it would dry. When it was dry, I folded it carefully and sat down under the linden tree again to wait for Josh and my brother to come out. Would I tell them what I had done?

I decided I would not. It would be better if Josh's surprise was real when his uncle looked at the order and saw only $20,000. Josh would be smart enough not to say he'd seen $200,000 on the order. And he'd honestly be able to verify that he'd heard his uncle dictate $200,000. The aide would be blamed. Who could prove it?

Like Josh had said, "Everybody has to do what they have to do."

When they came out, I handed Josh the folded note, and told him I was sorry, there was nothing I could think of to do. What could any of us do? He'd better get the note right to my father.

Sky and I walked with him to his horse. The street was deserted. "Maybe I'll see you all later," he said.

I thanked him for coming, and we stood watching him ride down the street. "Do you know what he had to do to be a courier?" Sky asked. "He had to join the army. His uncle made him take the oath and sign on."

"What?" I stared at my brother.

"Well, what'd you think? McCausland would let just anybody deliver such an important note? He's under his uncle's command now. In the army. He's a private."

I watched Josh receding down the street. Suddenly I was chilled. The sun was going down, wasn't it? I looked. It wasn't. It was still a bright red ball behind the trees.

CHAPTER EIGHTEEN

And I'll Never Be Able to Tell Anybody

We ate supper without Daddy. He'd sent a note around telling us that he was detained with special business. The young man who brought it said there were so many people milling around the courthouse that he could scarce get through the crowd. That Daddy and others were meeting, and maybe later Mama could send over some food.

I didn't see the note, but by now Mama knew what was going on. So did Aunt Lou, and probably Duke and Duchess, too. Word gets around in this town. Sky and I didn't have to say anything. The word "burn" was on nobody's lips in our house, but it was there, same as the chicken and potatoes, right at our supper table.

To say Aunt Lou was nervous was not to do justice

to what she was probably feeling. After she set down the food, she stood with her apron in her hands. "What does this mean?" she asked Mama.

Mama understood the question. And how, as it related to Aunt Lou, it was a different question than the one that had to do with the rest of us. "You're worried about the Rebels, aren't you?" she asked.

The woman did not answer. She could not bring herself to put her fears into words.

"We will not allow them to take you," Mama promised her. "I will personally see to that. But if you're still afraid, you may leave tonight. Pack. Take one of the horses and anything you need. Even if my husband doesn't go, you may leave. You've made the trip before, to and from Pennsylvania."

Aunt Lou was torn. She wanted to leave. Her fear of the Rebels was as a live thing in the room, like some cold mist swirling around her skirts. I could feel it around my own feet. Fear is terrible when it gets a grip on you. But she shook her head no. "I stay with you," she said.

Then came the question of who should bring supper to Daddy at the courthouse. Sky came alert instantly. "I'll take it, Mama."

She nodded slowly.

"Can I go, too?" I begged.

"No," Mama said. "I don't think the courthouse is any place for a girl right now, with all those Reb soldiers lounging around."

"Mama, I'm not a girl," I said.

"Oh? What are you, Amelia?"

"I mean, I'm not just any girl. I'm his daughter. Daddy's daughter. Please, Mama. I want to see Daddy. And I could be of help to Sky. Two of us together, we could look out for one another."

"How?" Mama asked.

I didn't know how. But I came up with something right quick. "Well, suppose a Reb soldier takes that dish of food away from Sky. Suppose they take Sky? I could run right back here and tell you."

"Suppose they take you?" There was a hint of amusement in her voice.

"They couldn't take the two of us," Sky said.

Mama smiled. "I suppose it's all right if you both go," she said. "The town is full of people we know. But don't get in the way of things, don't be a nuisance to your father and, oh yes, there is one more thing."

We waited.

"Aunt Lou, I think you should fix up a dish for General McCausland. We wouldn't want to cause any hard feelings. And it might help things along for my husband."

"Should be sendin' roast pheasant under glass, fricasseed oysters, and bonbons to that Southern general, if the reason is to save this town," Aunt Lou told us while she fixed two dishes of food in the kitchen. "Glazed ham, potatoes, and pole beans just ain't gonna do it."

I could see it vexed her to be sending a plate of food to a Rebel officer. It went against everything she stood for. But she set herself to the task nevertheless. She also sent a jug of cold cider.

"That ham is glazed just like your daddy likes it. Be careful, you two." She handed the jug of cider to Sky and the basket with the dishes in it to me. But first she put in two white, freshly laundered linen napkins. "That Southern general should know we're quality," she said.

The basket was heavy. Sky gave me the jug instead and took the basket in hand. Nobody paid mind to us on the streets. There were a lot of Rebel soldiers about. Cavalry. They lounged around on the wooden sidewalks, they leaned against hitching posts and in the doorways of boarded-up stores. They looked dusty and worn, for all the fine feathers cavalry wore. One thing we'd learned in this war. Cavalry, whether theirs or ours, was always trouble. They were cocky and arrogant. They thought the waters of all the rivers should part for them. And the citizens should not only be in awe of their wondrous deeds, but put up with their thieving ways. And then give fodder for their horses, too.

Two of them made outright nuisances of themselves as we were about to go by Mr. Hulsapple's Confectionary. Languidly, they walked right to the middle of the wooden sidewalk, barring our way.

"Excuse me, please," Sky said.

"Well, now, we'll have to study on it," one of them answered.

They were a ratty looking pair. And they smelled. Of horses, whiskey, and unwashed clothing.

"Whatever you got in that basket smells right good, little gal. Think you wanna share it?" His accent was so thick I could scarce make out the words.

Sky quickly moved to stand in front of me, on the other side. "It's for General McCausland," he said. "And my daddy. Supper. They're meeting at the courthouse. Now, if you wanna take it, go right ahead." Sky held out the basket.

They backed off. "No need to get huffy," one said. "It's just the smell. Near made me crazy. It ain't hardtack, that's for sure. You got any more of what's in that basket over to home?"

"Yes," Sky said. And told them how to get there.

They were the directions to the Dry Bridge on South Prospect Street. They thanked us and started off, thoughts of glazed ham and Aunt Lou's candied sweet potatoes dancing in their heads. We kept our heads down as the daylight got wider between us and them.

"Can't come back this way," Sky said. "They'll be waiting."

"You think they'll find our house, anyway?" I asked. "They know who our daddy is. Likely every Reb soldier in town knows by now."

"Nah," he said. "By tonight they'll be so drunk they won't care. Cavalry always drink. Count on it."

I was counting on a lot of things. Seeing Josh's red head in the crowd outside the courthouse, for instance. And when I didn't, when we'd pushed our way through the crowd, gone up the courthouse steps, and explained to the Rebel soldiers guarding the place who the food was for, I still didn't see Josh. My spirits fell.

A private, musket in hand, was ordered to take us to the clerk's office. There were soldiers all over the place in town hall, and they scowled at us as we went by. They may be cavalry, I thought, but they're a seedy lot. They looked wild and unkempt, like outlanders, like men who had done and seen it all, who had spent all their good chances, who would not hesitate to cut your throat for the time of day.

The private knocked on the door that said "City

Clerk." Someone called out that we should enter. The soldier opened the door.

They were around the desk, my daddy and the man I supposed to be General McCausland.

My daddy was talking. "It will be impossible to supply the clothing you request in this general order. The merchants have removed their stock from town."

McCausland looked awful young to be a general. But then, the only other Reb general I'd met was Robert E. Lee, who looked old and worn and sad. Yet Lee had been so polite, so gentlemanly.

McCausland was angry. "Then the town will be burned to the ground!" he growled.

I remembered that Josh had said this man was his mother's little brother. But he didn't look like any little brother to me. His hair was short, clipped around his ears, his nose long. Beneath it was a moustache that drooped down on the sides, to below his chin. His eyes were deep set and held such fire that they could fry you on the spot.

There was a paper on the desk between him and Daddy. Around them stood men I recognized from our town. Mr. Kausler was there. He was a teller at the Hagerstown Bank. J. Dixon Roman was the president of that bank. He'd recently broken his leg and was sitting in a straight-back chair, his crutches beside him. He looked to be in a great deal of pain, though whether that was from the leg or the demands of the Rebel general could not be determined. I thought that maybe he needed one of Aunt Lou's remedies. Will Hamilton and Isaac Nesbitt were there, too. And the town clerk. They all looked very sad.

McCausland looked up, saw us, and scowled. "Who are these children?" he demanded of the private.

The private near shook in his boots as he saluted. "Sir, they bring supper. Compliments of Mr. Grafton's wife, sir."

McCausland didn't know what all to do, then. He was embarrassed. Here he was, threatening to burn the town, and two children who lived in it stood there with offerings of food. You could smell the ham. The scent of it wafted through the room. "Set it down on a table there, Private."

There was a great deal of fussing as a table was cleared, the food set down. I took the moment to go to my daddy, who put out an arm and encircled my waist. "You all right?" I asked.

"I'm fine, Amelia. Tell your mother I'm just fine."

"Aunt Lou says you're not to let the food get cold. It's glazed ham, candied potatoes, and pole beans.

She said she wishes she had roast pheasant, fricasseed oysters, and bonbons, but this is the best she could do on such short notice."

"To us it'll taste like roast pheasant, at least," Daddy said.

McCausland cleared his throat. "Do you think we can finish this waltz and get on with the negotiations?" he asked gruffly.

"Why don't you two get on home," Daddy suggested gently.

We said yes. Daddy had his hand in mine, and as I moved away from him I didn't want to let his hand go. It was so warm and safe-feeling. He looked tired, too, but he was smiling, trying to keep everybody's spirits from getting cast down.

Tears came to my eyes. I didn't want to leave him here like this, with this evil man who had eyes that could fry you. It wasn't fair that the whole burden of things should be on my father. People had talked so about his making money on the war. Insulted Mama about it. Where were those people now? Gone. Fled. Skedaddled. Like Mayor Ratliff. And here was my father, trying to do right for all of them, in his gentle, becalming way.

There were tears in my eyes when I walked to the door. And then McCausland's voice stopped us. "Wait."

We waited. Everybody did.

"For some godforsaken reason that nobody has yet explained to me, this order requests twenty thousand dollars instead of two hundred thousand. Before this war is over, the brass-bound fool who did this will pay."

His eyes, deep and accusing, went around the room. They stopped and bore into me. And I knew in that moment that God could not put more terror into me. The enormity of what I had done came over me. This man was a high-ranking Confederate officer, a man accustomed to killing. He had killed, and he would kill again. It was the business he was about, his reason for being. His boots were worn down from the miles he had traveled to do this killing, his uniform dusty, his face worn. And around him were his men, looking even worse than him.

And I, a mere girl, had taken a paintbrush in some fanciful moment and removed a zero on the amount of money from his official order. I supposed a soldier could hang for something like that.

He spoke now, again. "But there is no reason for me to accept less than the amount of clothing and supplies I requisitioned. You have four hours to deliver it."

I saw Daddy nod in compliance. "Four hours," he said.

"Is there any reason why these two children can't start collecting items? And tell your neighbors?"

Daddy looked a bit startled at first, then reined himself in. "No," he said, "no reason. You hear that, Amelia? Sky? We have four hours. Get the word out on our street. We need clothing, especially shoes, hats, coats, and trousers. Sky, here's the key to the store. You'll find some of the items we need in crates. You know where." He reached into his coat pocket, drew it out, and tossed it to Sky, who caught it.

"Yessir," Sky said. "Come, Amelia, we've work to do."

As the doors closed behind us, I heard McCausland roar. "Four hours, Grafton, no more! Or the town burns!" The man was near to apoplexy. He needed a good dose of Aunt Lou's tonic.

Everyone was scurrying around the halls of the courthouse as we were ushered out by the private. Outside, the soldiers were reading the demands to the town folk, who were still milling around, waiting for word of what would happen. You could hear the murmurs of dismay from the people in the crowd. Four hours! They broke away, one by one, heading into the darkness, home.

Sky grabbed my arm. "Do you think we can do it? Come up with what he needs?"

"I don't see why not."

"He wouldn't burn the town. He just wouldn't. Do you think?"

"I think he is evil," I said. "And yes, I think he would." I was shivering. Never had I been so frightened as when that man looked at me and said he would find the person who'd changed the figures on his order! Could he find out? Was there some way? Did officers have special powers?

More to the point, did Josh suspect me? And could he be made to tell I'd had the note in my hands?

As Sky and I rushed home to get the horse and wagon and drive it to the store, I stayed frightened. I wondered where Josh was. And whether he would point a finger at me if questioned. And what I would do if he did. We passed scurrying groups of people headed to the courthouse with bundles of clothing in their hands, and it came to me that our town could be saved. We just might be able to get together the clothing. We would be able to afford $20,000.

Likely, I had helped save it.

But I was still frightened.

I had done something, finally, in this war. Something worthwhile. Why didn't I feel elated? And then I thought of Jinny Pearl, and wondered if she was on a battlefield somewhere, knowing she was doing something good, but still frightened.

Doing something good doesn't keep you from fear,

I decided. And that wasn't right. I'd always thought doing something good should make you righteous. And with such righteousness, should come pride. And courage. I felt cheated.

But if I was cheated, so were lots of others. But what about those like McCausland, who did evil? How did they feel?

I thought about Jinny Pearl again and what she had once told me. "I can't pretend the war doesn't exist. I have to do something. Sooner or later, we all have to. It isn't your time yet, is all. When the time comes, you'll know it."

I had known it. And done something. I was the brass-bound fool who'd changed that $200,000 into $20,000. And I would never, as long as I lived, be able to tell anybody.

CHAPTER NINETEEN

Final Payment

After four trips with the wagon from Daddy's store to the courthouse that night, Sky and I went home. At the end of our street, Sky nudged me.

"Look at that, Amelia."

I looked. There, in the open field just past our house, were several Reb soldiers, hauling bundles of twigs and kindling wood, and gathering pine-knot torches.

"They aim to burn the town, all right," Sky said. "And they're gonna start at this end. With our house."

Terror gripped me. When we got to our front gate, I turned to see the last purple light over Elk Ridge. Up there in the mountains there would still be some light left in places. Here it was dark, but for tiny pin-pricks of light from the house windows. The town seemed so peaceful from here. "It's a beautiful town, Sky," I said.

"Thought you hated it."

"I don't anymore."

"Yeah, well, I gotta get this horse some water. Still gotta deliver our things to the courthouse."

I nodded. "I'll go inside and see if Aunt Lou has everything ready."

Aunt Lou was in the parlor, surrounded by piles of men's clothing. "I didn't know we had that much in the house," I said.

She gave me one of those sidelong glances that showed mostly the whites of her eyes. "They'd be more if'n your mama would give the rest."

"What rest?"

"Mebbe you could talk to her. She's got it upstairs. Your brother Wes's clothes. Likely he's outgrown 'em already, but she won't give 'em over."

The way she said it bespoke concern, more than for Wes's clothes. I ran up the stairs.

A lamp was lit in Wes's room. There I found my mother, in the middle of Wes's bed, surrounded by piles of his clothing.

"Mama, what are you doing?"

She seemed fine. She smiled. "I suppose you could say I'm guarding these things from Aunt Lou. She wants to give them away."

I walked into the room. "We need them, Mama. If the Rebels don't get enough clothing and boots, they're going to burn the town."

"Did Sky give his good trousers and jacket?" she asked.

"He said he was going to."

"Well, whatever will he wear to church on Sunday? Did he think of that?"

She did not understand what was going on. How could she not? "Mama," I said gently, "there will be no church left to go to on Sunday if we don't give them what they want."

She picked up some long socks of Wes's and rolled them in a ball. "These are all the clothes Wes has, excepting for his uniform. And from what he writes, that's near in shreds. What will he wear when he comes home?"

"You've plenty of time to get him more clothes before then, Mama. Please." I stepped forward. "We really need the clothes. Everybody in town's been trekking to the courthouse with clothing. And I saw Mrs. Jones. Travis and Cole's mother. She brought all their clothing, and you know how poor they are. Besides, Daddy is working so hard to save the town. Can't you understand?"

"I do understand, Amelia." She looked at me. "But I can't give Wes's clothes. I have this feeling that if I do, I'm admitting he'll never have use for them again. I can't do that. I have to keep his clothing. That way, I know he'll be back. So please, take anything you want of your father's or Sky's. But Wes's clothing stays right here. They can burn the town around it."

I felt so helpless. I just stood there, like a jackass in the rain. Then I had a thought. "Mama, did you ever think that maybe Wes would want you to do it?"

She didn't answer. And in the next instant, I heard someone coming up the stairs. Two someones.

Mama and I both waited to see who it was.

In another moment, Sky stood in the doorway. "Mama, there's someone here to see you," he said. Then he stepped aside.

It was Aunt Charlotte. Mama's face lit up, and she stood to greet her, holding out her hands. "Where have you been?"

Aunt Charlotte came into the room, holding a burlap bag. "I was visiting my sister in Ohio for a while. I got back last week. I was going to come see you. And now this." She set the bag down and she and Mama hugged. Then Aunt Charlotte pointed to the burlap bag. "I brought back your tea set," she said. "I kept it well hidden for you. But now I'm afraid those rascals will come around to my place and take it. I don't want to be responsible for it anymore, Leigh."

Mama got off the bed to kneel on the floor and open the burlap sack. Slowly, she took out the contents. One by one, she laid the shining pieces on the floor, the precious tea set that was brought from England by her great-grandmother, all of a piece. Aunt Charlotte had it polished to a fare-thee-well, too.

"You want me to take it back and hide it again, Leigh, just say the word," Aunt Charlotte said.

Mama just knelt there, picking up every piece of the set, running her hands over the pieces lovingly. "No, Aunt Charlotte," she said. "I don't want you to take it back and hide it. It's the grace of God that brought you to us just now."

Aunt Charlotte looked confused.

Mama stood up and hugged her again. "How'd you get here?"

"Walked."

"With all those Reb soldiers about? Weren't you worried?"

"I'd have hit them with the burlap bag if they'd bothered me," Aunt Charlotte said. "Knocked them out."

"Well, I'll have Sky walk you home."

"No need. If I can't handle a few Reb soldiers, I'm not worth my salt," Aunt Charlotte said. "It's good seeing you again, Leigh. I'm home to stay. When this is over, I'll be bringing my vegetables and fruits around again."

They agreed how nice that would be, and Aunt Charlotte left. When she was gone down the stairs, Sky and I just stared at Mama. She was kneeling again, shoving the pieces of the tea set back into the burlap sack. Then she picked up the sack and handed it to Sky.

"You give this to the Rebel general, son," she said.

Sky backed away, not taking the sack.

"Mama, you can't!" I said.

"Oh? And why can't I?"

"Because, it's your great-grandma's tea service that she saved when she had to throw everything else off that wagon! Because it's your most prized possession!"

She smiled, set the sack down again, and reached out to touch my face. "My children are my most prized possession," she said softly. "Your father, this town, and the people in it are my most prized possession."

"But you wouldn't give Wes's clothes!"

"No. They are important to me. More important than this tea service. Now, will you and Sky bring it to the courthouse? Or must I?"

I took the sack up from the floor.

"And tell your father I'll keep a light in the window for him."

"Come on, Sky," I said.

Outside our house, the Reb soldiers, with their piles of twigs, their kindling, their pine-knot torches, waited. They waited at every corner in town, as Sky and I walked quickly past them with our booty.

Gaslight cast eerie shadows on the streets. The piles of goods brought by the people were guarded by Rebel soldiers under arms, with more stationed around the courthouse. Sky and I knew that Daddy and the men were still inside, working out the final arrangements to save the town.

We tried to go up the courthouse steps, but a sentry stopped us. "Can't go inside now. Important meeting going on."

"I've got something valuable here for General McCausland," Sky told him. "It's worth a lot of money."

The sentry peered into the burlap sack and gave out a low whistle. "Take it over to the captain, there by the door," he directed.

We walked over to the captain, and Sky told him the same thing. He looked bored and tired, but he looked into the sack, then at us with no expression on his face. "If it was a side of roast ham and a pint of whiskey, now, that would be worth something," he said.

"It's my mother's good tea set. An heirloom," I said. I grabbed the sack from Sky. "I want to bring it inside now. Unless you people don't want it."

"Easy there, missy. I'll have someone bring it in."

"I'll bring it in," I said. "It was a great sacrifice for my mother to give it. I'll see it safely inside. My name is Amelia Grafton. This is my brother Schuyler. Our father is in there, negotiating with McCausland."

The captain shrugged and still managed to look bored. "All right, go on in. Three minutes. You got three minutes. No, you stay here," he said to Sky. "This isn't a family reunion."

I went in the door and down the hall. More sentries. But when they saw me lugging the sack, one came forward and offered to help.

"I have to bring it inside," I said. "It's important. My father is Mr. Grafton. He's inside."

He looked over my shoulder, and when I turned, I saw the sentry at the door waving that it was all right. "Let me carry it for you, little missy," he said.

"If you just open the door, I think I want to bring it in myself," I told him.

He did so.

Everybody inside looked up. I saw the surprise on Daddy's face that I was back again. Or that I was dragging a burlap sack, struggling with it for all I was worth.

I straightened up. I did not look at my father. I looked at McCausland. "It's my great-great-grandmother's silver tea set," I told him. "She brought it from England. Her ship ran into a gale and ran off course, and had to drop anchor in Maine. She traveled by ox-drawn wagon to Boston, and because the roads were so steeped in mud, she had to discard most of her things. But she kept this tea set."

He said nothing. His mouth was open. I knew the spectacle I made, standing there with my hair hanging and my clothes in disarray from the night's exertions.

"Now it's yours," I told him. "Just don't burn our town."

McCausland nodded to an aide, who came forward and opened the sack, then whistled. "Looks like this might bring the money up to snuff, Sir," he said.

McCausland nodded, and the aide dragged the sack into a corner. McCausland looked at me, again with those piercing eyes.

I returned the look, no longer afraid. I didn't go to my father this time to be hugged. I just smiled at him. "Everything is fine at home, Daddy," I said. "Mama says she'll keep a light in the window for you."

He nodded in approval. I saw a twinkle in his eyes, and something of relief on his face as the thoughts came together in his head about the tea set and what it was worth, and how it would help things.

I went out of the room and out into the hallway, feeling a bursting of pride. I walked quickly down the hallway and out into the night to where Sky was waiting.

CHAPTER TWENTY

Two Letters

NOVEMBER 24, 1864

In October Atlanta was captured, and in November President Lincoln got himself re-elected. Daddy said it was the first time in history that armies of a major nation would vote during a war.

One of the first things Lincoln did was declare a day of national thanksgiving. People in Hagerstown knew they had a lot to be thankful for this year, even if some of them did return to town to make a fuss because the ransom money was paid. It'll take years to pay the debt off, they yelled.

Jacob Wright found himself in the unusual position of defending my daddy as one of the men who had saved the town. He had to. His name was on a paper that Daddy had important people sign to show they agreed with him about what was done with the ransom.

That was a right fine idea of Daddy's, that paper. Because of it, the state assembly said the town could issue bonds. Which meant the debt was now on the tax bills, under the heading of "the McCausland debt."

We all had a little part of it. Even though some had already paid more than they could stand to do. My friend Josh, for instance. And Mama, with her tea set. And me. Nobody will ever know what some of us had paid, not that you can compare a tea set to what Josh did. Even if it did come over from England from my great-great-grandmother.

In church this official Thanksgiving day, I had two letters in my dress pocket. I knew them both by heart, I'd read them so often.

One was from Josh. It was dated the end of August.

It read:

Dear Amelia:

I'm sorry I was not able to see you again after that night, but my uncle signed me on that day he made me courier, so I had to report back to camp immediately. When I heard how all fired up he was about what happened with the general order, I put two and two together and figured what had happened.

Well, Amelia, I never would have believed it of

you. So I see you finally decided to do something about the war. Well, you did it, all right. It makes anything I've done seem pale in comparison. I'm so proud of you.

When I was questioned, I lied my head off, of course. I told him it said twenty thousand when it was handed to me. So he went on to question others. The matter has not yet been resolved. Perhaps it never will be.

So I am now a private in his cavalry. My uncle has outfitted me. You should see me. I have all I can do to keep my glasses from falling off my nose when I ride with them. But I figure this will be a good opportunity to collect more information, firsthand.

Don't worry about me, I am fine. I can't tell you where I am, but I know that by now you heard about how my uncle had the town of Chambersburg burned the last week in July. This time, he wanted five hundred thousand in currency, or one hundred thousand in gold. The town folk couldn't raise that kind of money, so he left the town in flames. It was not a sight I shall ever forget, I can tell you.

On August first, we were in Hancock, Pennsylvania. Here my uncle asked for thirty thousand, or the town would burn. It was just a small river town. My uncle said he didn't care. But two of his officers — Major Gilmore and General Johnson — did. They argued with him. Johnson actually went against his orders and ordered two battalions into Hancock to protect the people. I went along with him. My uncle cannot forgive me for that, but I don't much care. I am staying under Johnson's command. When this war is over, I want people to know there were some good men in the South. Just as there are some bad men in the North. It isn't all simple as it sometimes seems.

I will write again when I get the chance. I'm having a fine time, don't worry about me. I haven't actually had to kill anybody yet. So I'm not going against my principles.

Your good friend, always,
JOSH DECHART

The second letter was from Johnson, the officer of McCausland, whom Josh had continued to serve under. It was dated the end of August.

Dear Miss Grafton:
It is my sad duty to inform you that Private Joshua Dechart, who served under my command, was fatally wounded in a skirmish in Moorefield, Virginia, where we engaged Brigadier General

William Averell's 3rd Pennsylvania Cavalry. They had been steadily pursuing us since we left Hancock.

Your friend, Private Dechart, asked me to write to you if anything happened to him in battle. So I write this note at his request.

He fought bravely, and with fortitude. He never sought special treatment or shied away from dangerous situations because he was a nephew of McCausland, even though I know he had a personal distaste for this war. At Hancock he stood by me when I ordered two battalions to protect the people, incurring the wrath of his uncle.

I am sorry to have to write of his demise. We made him as comfortable as we could before he died. At this time, he asked me to forward to you his notes, which he took while he served with us. I enclose them here.

I leave it to you to inform his people. Please let me extend my condolences and my wishes that this war will soon be over.

SIGNED:

BRIGADIER GENERAL BRADLEY TYLER JOHNSON

CONFEDERATE STATES OF AMERICA

Enclosed were notes Josh had taken about serving in the Confederate cavalry. And some pencil sketches of the men he had served with. They were very good.

Sometime After the End
of the War, 1865

Nobody ever found out who changed the amount of money on that general order from Brigadier General McCausland. And, as far as I'm concerned, nobody ever will.

The money that saved Hagerstown came from two of our banks, and one in nearby Williamsport. Daddy says they will be years getting it back.

Josh's old newspaper office still sits, all boarded up, with the sign hanging on one hinge. I don't pass by if I can help it. I can't bear to. I still think that if I go around to the back door and give my special knock, Josh will answer, open the door, and invite me in. I still see him in his leather apprentice's apron, his hands all smudged with printers' ink.

He didn't have to be in the army. He never wanted to. He agreed to be courier for his uncle so he could show us that general order. He did it for me. And he couldn't be courier unless he signed on.

My brother Wes returned to us all of a piece. He was mustered out as soon as the war ended in April. He goes back to St. James College this fall. Sky will be going there, too. Wes has gotten taller and thinner. He doesn't fit in all those clothes Mama saved for him anymore. They had to be given away to charity. I will be going to the Female Seminary.

Mama had a baby girl in February. She is named Mary Louise, after my great-great-grandmother, whose tea set Mama gave to McCausland. Mama says a baby is better than an old tea set, any day. It's odd to have a baby in the house, but it's also nice. Daddy says Mama looks as young as she did when Wes was born. Mary Louise is very cunning, and we all spoil her very much. But sometimes I think how she'll never know what it was like to live through the war. I'll have to tell her. And that will separate her from the rest of us, because the war has marked us all so.

Jinny Pearl returned home, too. The story that is being given around is that she went off to Washington City, to help be a nurse to the wounded. She and Wes are friends, but not sweethearts anymore. Jinny says they can't be. Though they were both in the war, she was in more battles than he.

"I bested him in so many things," she told me. "How can we marry? He'll never forgive me."

But I think it's more than that. I think it's that she can't stay around here anymore. Not after the things she's seen. "I can't go back to my old life," she said. "I can't abide the farm. I want to go to Oregon or California."

There are times I lie awake nights and think how it would have been if I hadn't tampered with that general order. Our town would have been burned. Like Chambersburg. The people there had to flee to the cemetery. McCausland burned four hundred buildings, and near three hundred of them were homes. The place was in ruins.

One elderly lady beat a Rebel soldier with a broom when he wanted to put the torch to her house. He ran. I suppose we all fought the war in our own way.

I feel so proud when I think of what my war turned out to be. Then I think of Josh. And how I couldn't have done it unless he'd come back with that general order. But look what the price for that turned out to be, in the end: his life.

Oh, my head goes round and round in circles thinking of it. Then, every so often, I get a whole new idea about it. And I think, "I'll run down to the news-paper office and tell Josh." And then I remember.

There is no way out of it for me. I keep going around in circles.

I know my daddy is having the same trouble with what he did. Sometimes I hear Mama and Daddy talking about the ransom of Hagerstown. Because some people still complain about the McCausland debt on their taxes. "Our children will be paying it off," they complain.

And even though others in town were there with him, negotiating, I know Daddy still holds himself responsible. Because lots of people complained that it wasn't right to pay the money to the Rebels.

"The most important thing we ever have to learn in life is to live with our choices," Mama tells him.

"You make a choice," Daddy says, "and you pay for it the rest of your life. In this case, everybody in town is paying. Don't think that doesn't bother me, Leigh."

Daddy is right. You make a choice and you pay. Worse yet, sometimes other people pay. Even though the choice you made is right.

And then there is this: I shall always be paying my own installments on the McCausland debt.

This novel is based on the ransom of Hagerstown, Maryland, which happened in the first week of July, 1864, when Confederate Brigadier General John McCausland, acting under orders from General Jubal Early, set out to demand two hundred thousand dollars from the town and threatened to burn it if the money wasn't delivered.

Somehow — and history never tells us how — a tenth of that amount was written on the general order that was given to town officials. And the town fathers of Hagerstown were able to redeem their town for twenty thousand and an exact number of coats, pants, shoes, shirts, hats, and other pieces of clothing demanded by McCausland.

This is the basis of my novel, the nucleus on which the story was planned.

The Grafton family is fictitious. However, the town treasurer, Matthew S. Barber, did head up the committee that negotiated with McCausland, and Hagerstown did meet the ransom.

Josh Dechart is a fictional character, although Daniel Dechart, editor of the *Hagerstown Mail*, a newspaper with Confederate leanings, did spend six weeks in a Federal prison for his writings, and his equipment was later smashed by an angry mob. Dechart did flee Hagerstown.

Many of the characters in this book, however, did actually live in town at the time, and I found them in S. Roger Keller's wonderful account of Hagerstown during the Civil War, *Events of the Civil War in Washington County, Maryland*, and in his *Crossroads of War*, which tells the stories of many of Hagerstown's citizens.

In most instances, I used events that really happened to these characters. For instance, Dewitt Clinton Rench was shot and killed by a mob in Williamsport before leaving to join the Confederate army. Lutie Kealhofer was the belle of the town and did, for the most part, play the role I have her playing. There was an Aunt Charlotte who delivered fresh fruits and vegetables, and the battles and skirmishes that I have happening in town are accurate, as is the role of General Robert E. Lee in my novel. Many other minor characters in the book had things happen to them exactly as I have written.

Jinny Pearl Beale is fictional, although a young lady in nearby Williamsport was so bothered by a Rebel picket that she shot and killed him, and members of her family helped her hide the body. This event gave me the basis for Jinny Pearl. I then added the dimension of "female soldier," since quite a few served in the Civil War under the disguise of men.

With the exception of Amelia's father's store, all other business establishments, churches, schools, and Civil War hospitals in town are accurately depicted. Every movement of both armies, every battle, every military history occurrence, is documented and correct.

Hagerstown was strife-torn throughout the war. It was invaded three times by Lee's army. Southerners came through for the Battle of Antietam in 1863, again on their way to Gettysburg, and again in 1864, when the town was held for ransom by the South. In between there were endless skirmishes. One army or another was always coming through, which meant not only confusion and fear for the residents, but the depletion of their resources, as armies are always hungry and in need of food and supplies.

Then, after Gettysburg in 1863, there was a battle in the town itself, before Lee pulled his Confederates out and back across the flood-swollen Potomac River.

Indeed, all of Washington County, Maryland, suffered tremendous losses and destruction during this war, which means Clear Springs, Funkstown, Williamsport, Boonsboro, and other small towns, as well.

Still, Maryland remained strong for the Union. It was a crucial state for President Lincoln, although many of its inhabitants were pro-South. This meant bad feelings of one neighbor for the other. Hagerstown did indeed have its Jacob Wrights, who were just waiting for the right moment to inform the Confederates about their staunch Union neighbors, and so many an old quarrel or feud was "settled" under this guise of patriotism.

But remember, this is a work of historical fiction. I took the history I had — and the wonderful fact that to this day, nobody really knows how that two hundred thousand dollars in General Early's order got changed to twenty thousand — and built my story around it.

Faust, L. Patricia. ed. *Historical Times Illustrated Encyclopedia of the Civil War.* New York: Harper and Row Publishers, 1986.

Hall, Richard. *Patriots in Disguise, Women Warriors of the Civil War.* New York: Marlowe and Company, 1993.

Keller, Roger S. *Crossroads of War: Washington County, Maryland in the Civil War.* Shippensburg, Pennsylvania: The Burd Street Press, 1997.

———. *Events of the Civil War in Washington County, Maryland.* Shippensburg, Pennsylvania: The Burd Street Press, 1995.

Long, E. B., and Barbara Long. *The Civil War Day by Day.* New York: Da Capo Press, 1971.

Massey, Mary Elizabeth. *Ersatz in the Confederacy: Shortages and Substitutes on the Southern Homefront.* Columbia, South Carolina: University of South Carolina Press, 1952.

McDonald, Cornelia Peake. *A Woman's Civil War, A Diary with Reminiscences of the War, from March 1862.* Madison, Wisconsin: The University of Wisconsin Press, 1992.

Murfin, James. "Lee's Lost Orders," Gettysburg, Pa., *Civil War Times,* vol. 1, no. 5 (August 1962).

Naisawald, L. Van Loan. "Why Confederates Invaded Maryland." *Civil War Times,* vol. 1, no. 5 (August 1962).

Saxe, Stephen O. *American Iron Hand Presses: The Story of the Iron Hand Press in America.* New Castle, Delaware: Oak Knoll Books, 1992.

Stinson, Dwight E., Jr. "The Battle of South Mountain," *Civil War Times,* vol. 1, no. 5 (August 1962).